BEAN

The Stretchy Dragon

Ari Stocrate

Andrews McMeel
PUBLISHING®

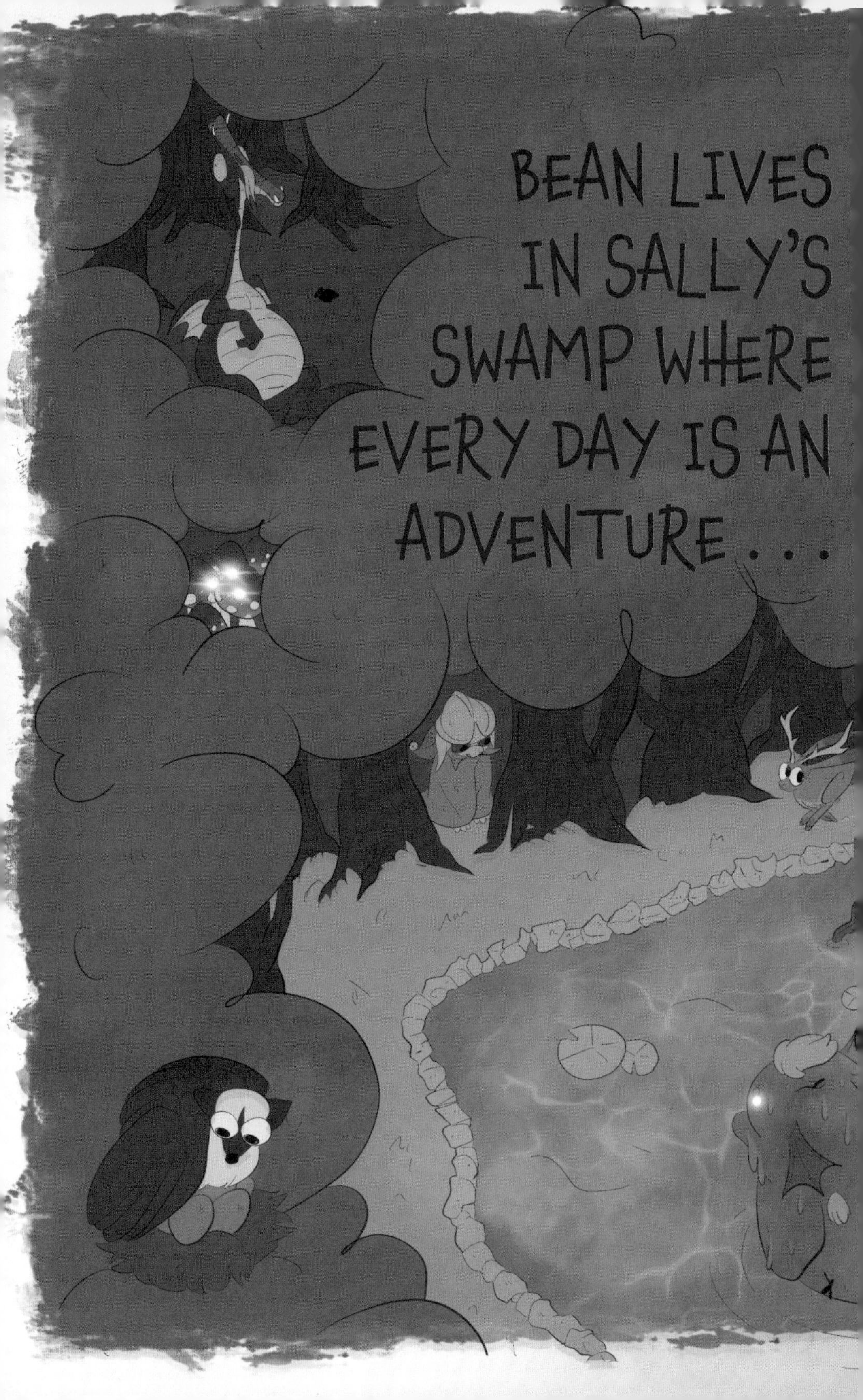
BEAN LIVES IN SALLY'S SWAMP WHERE EVERY DAY IS AN ADVENTURE . . .

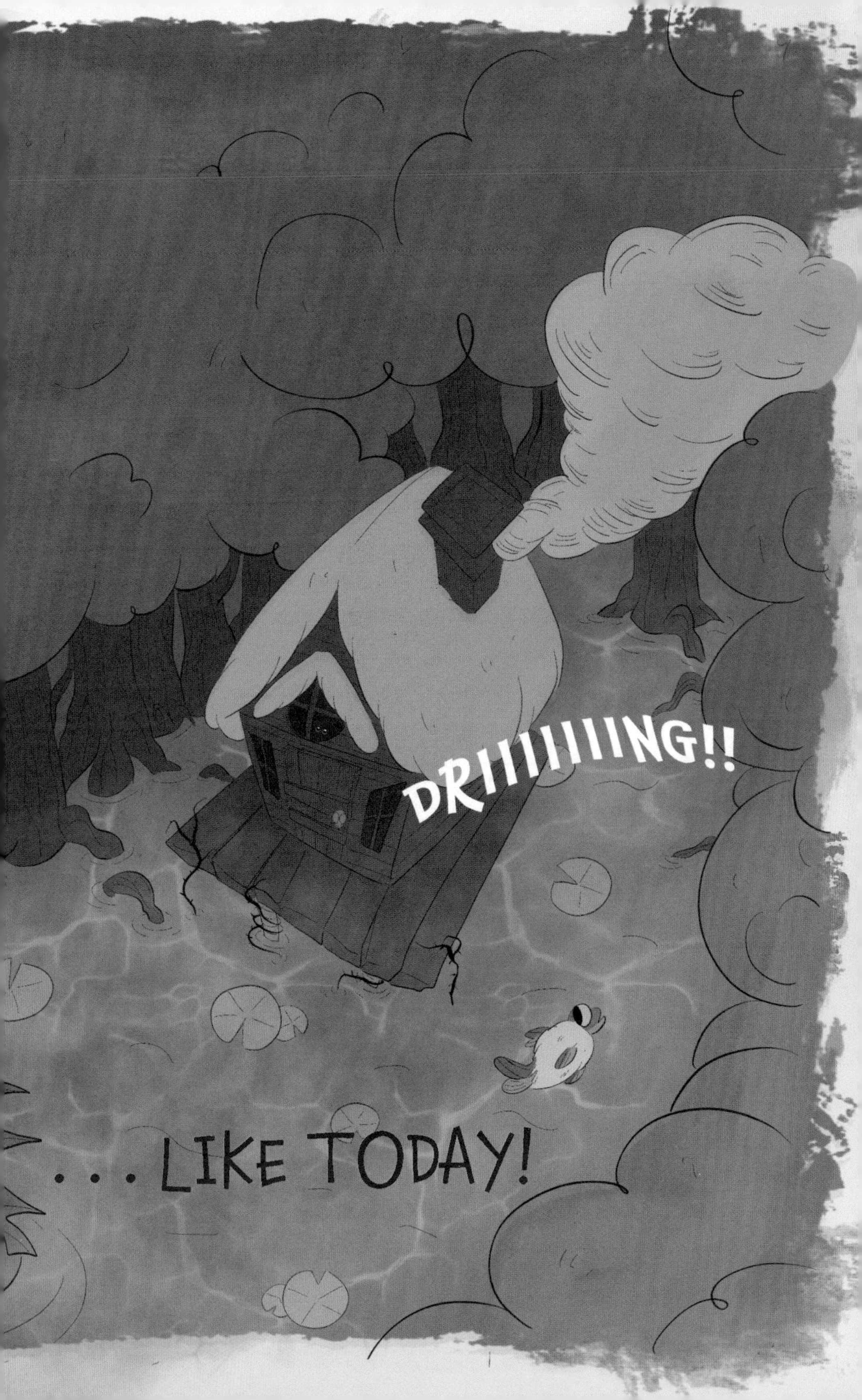
DRIIIIIIING!!
. . . LIKE TODAY!

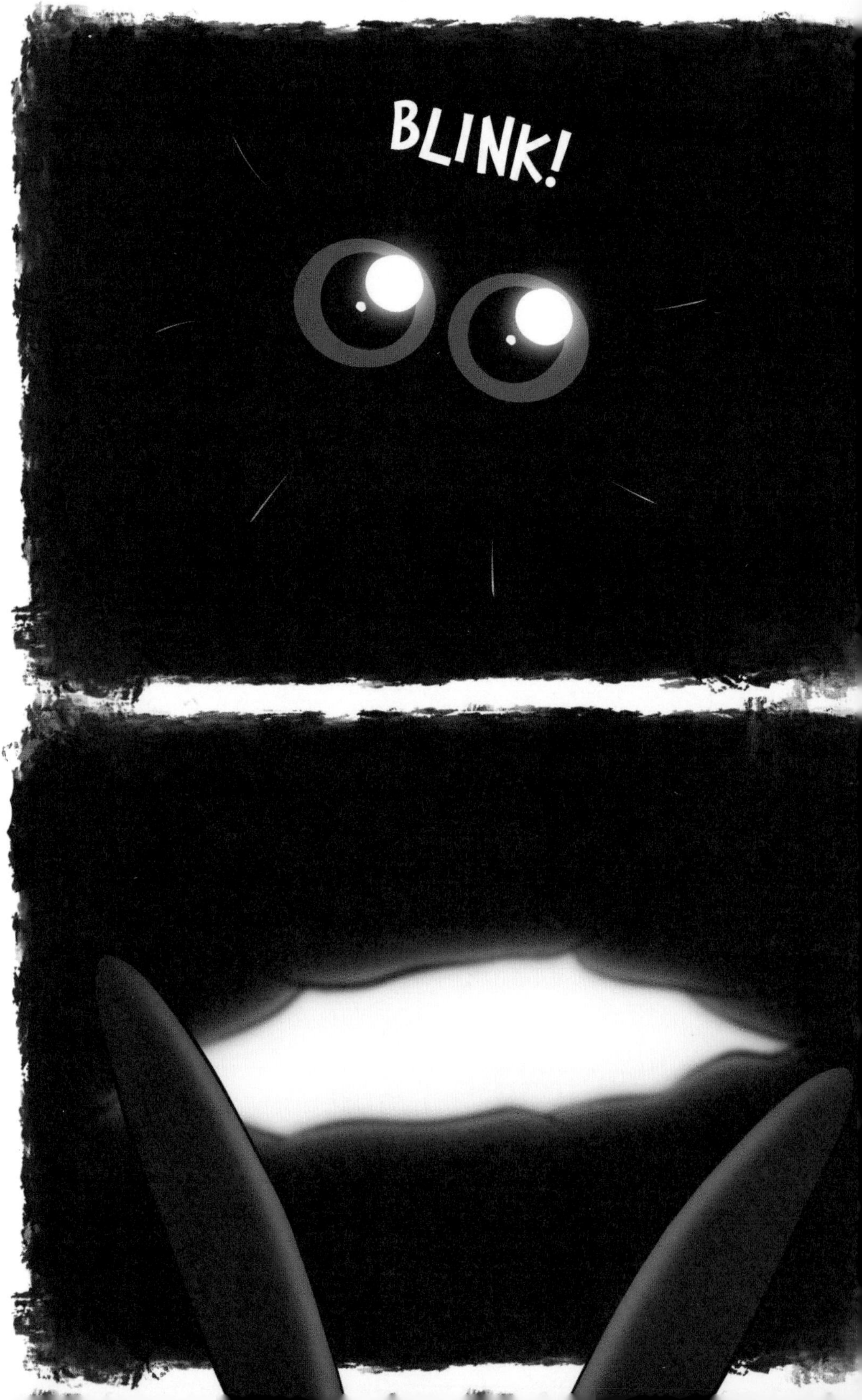
BLINK!

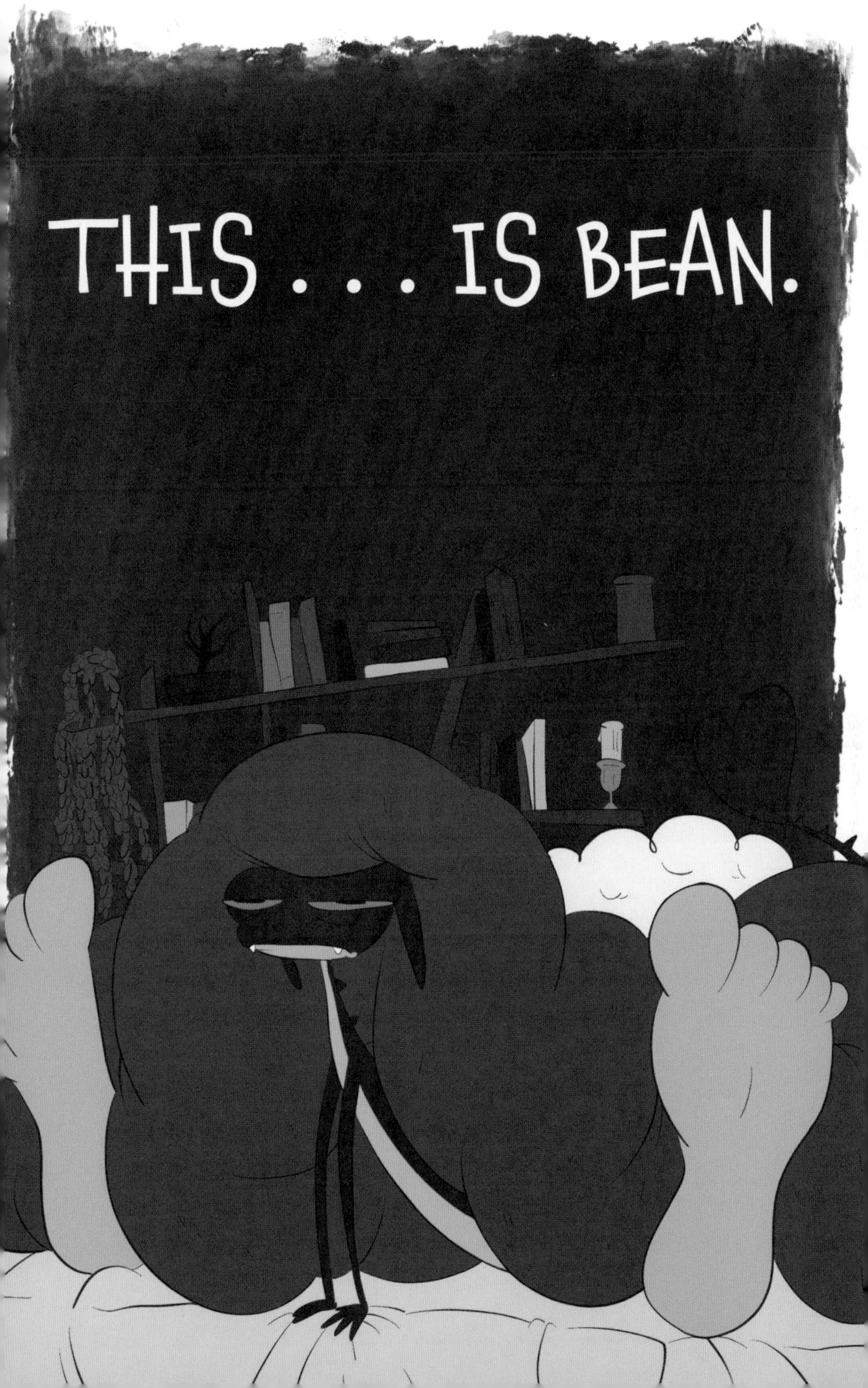
THIS . . . IS BEAN.

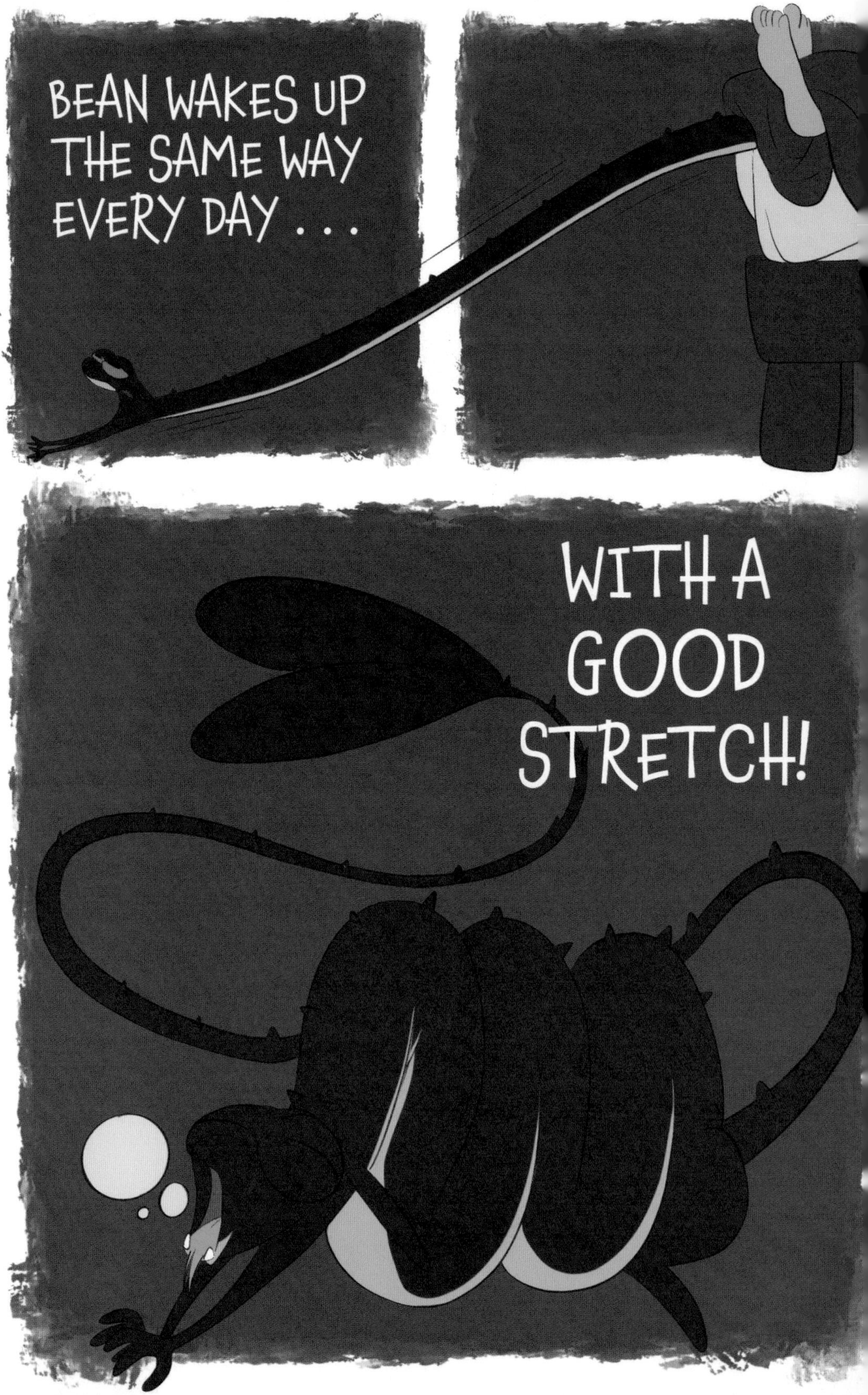
BEAN WAKES UP THE SAME WAY EVERY DAY . . .
WITH A GOOD STRETCH!

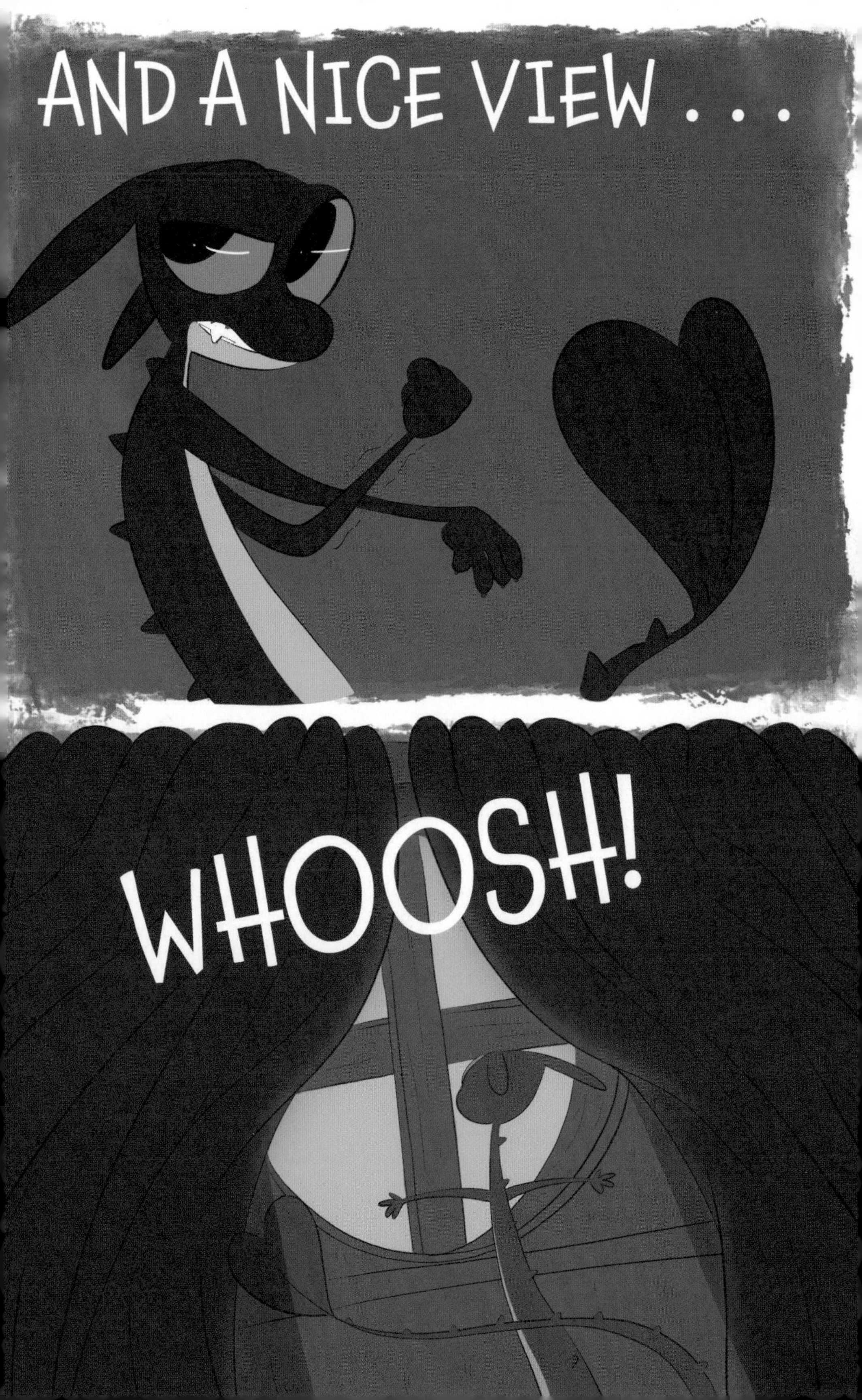
AND A NICE VIEW . . .
WHOOSH!

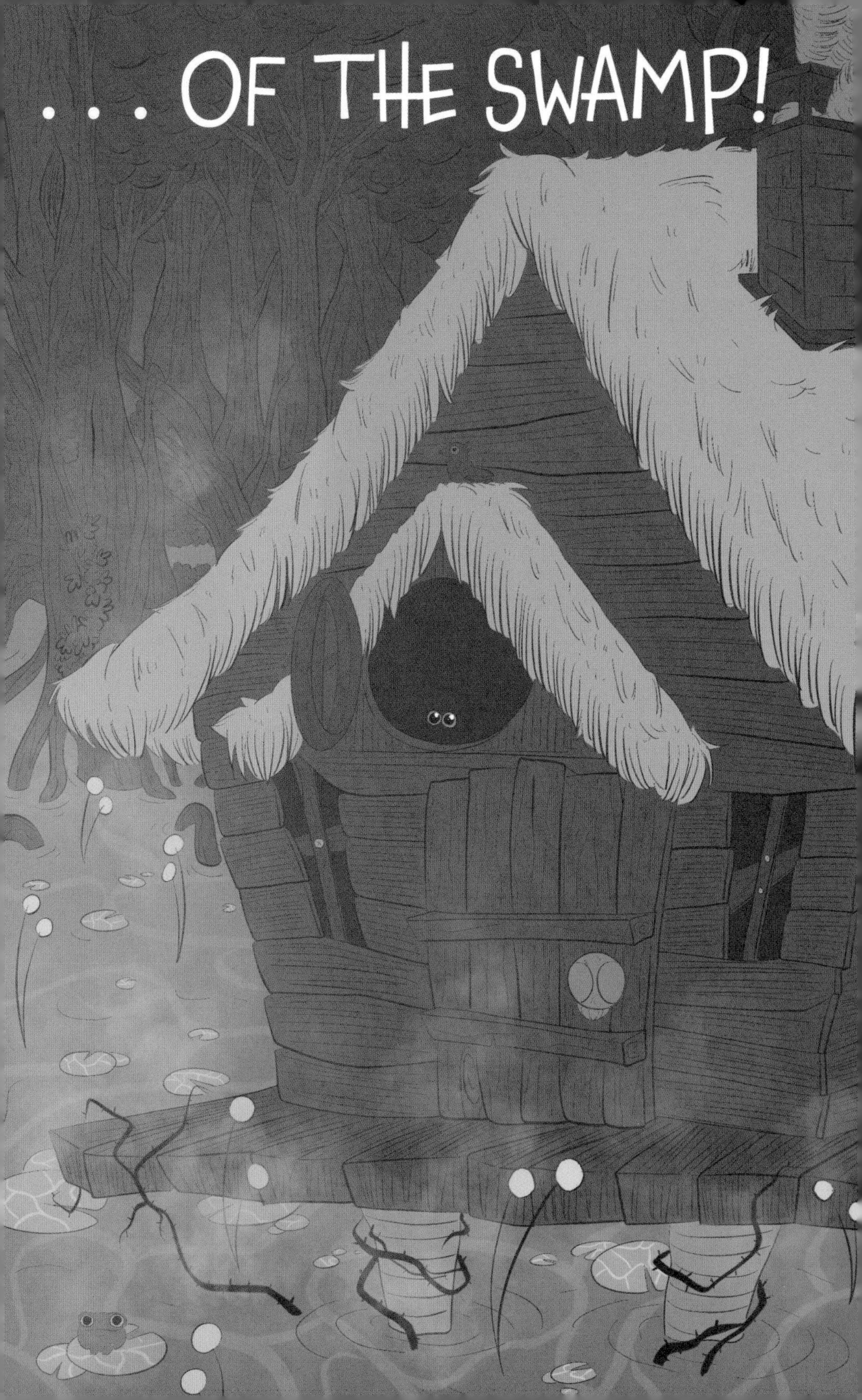
. . . OF THE SWAMP!

BEAN TUMBLES DOWNSTAIRS.

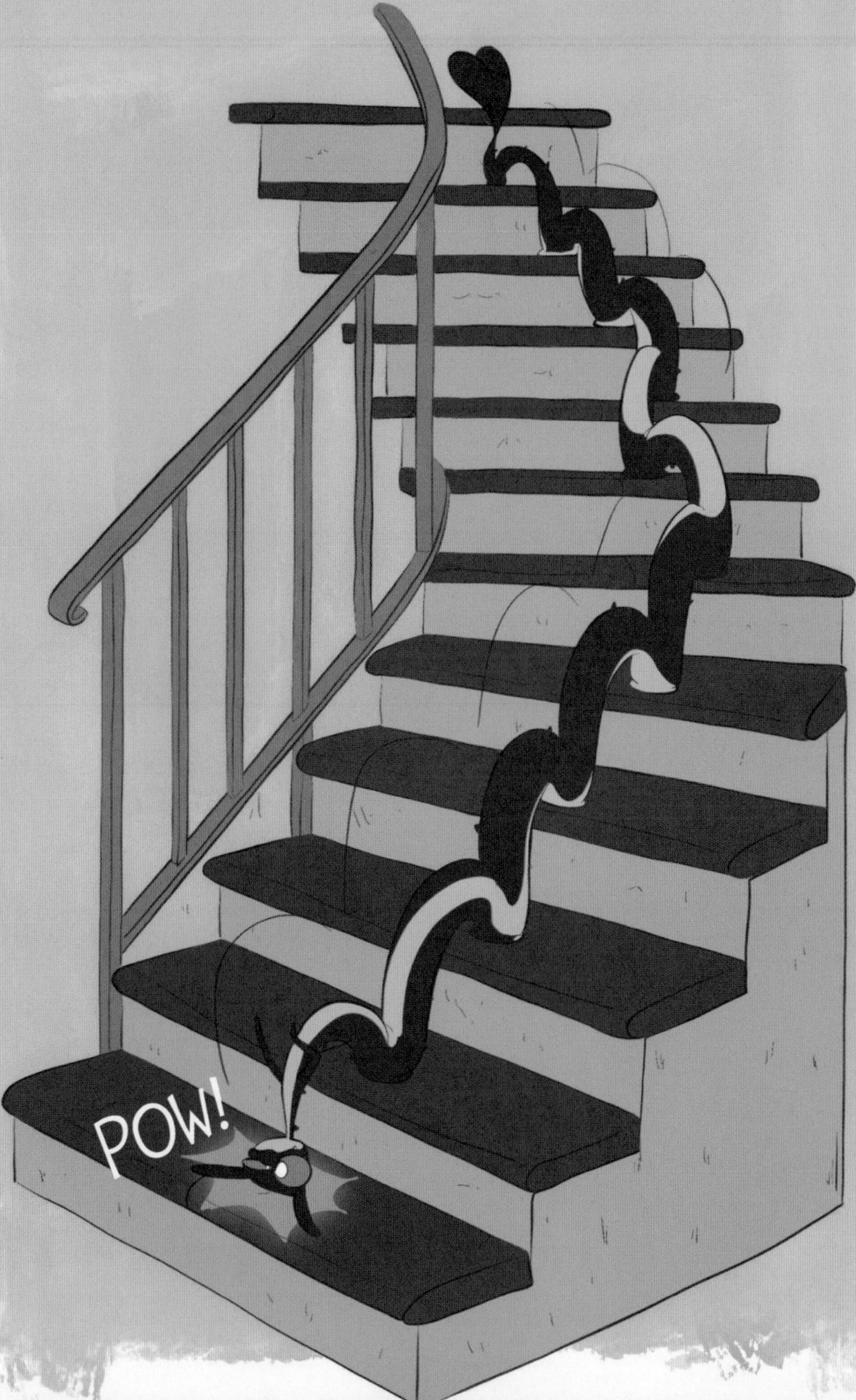
POW!

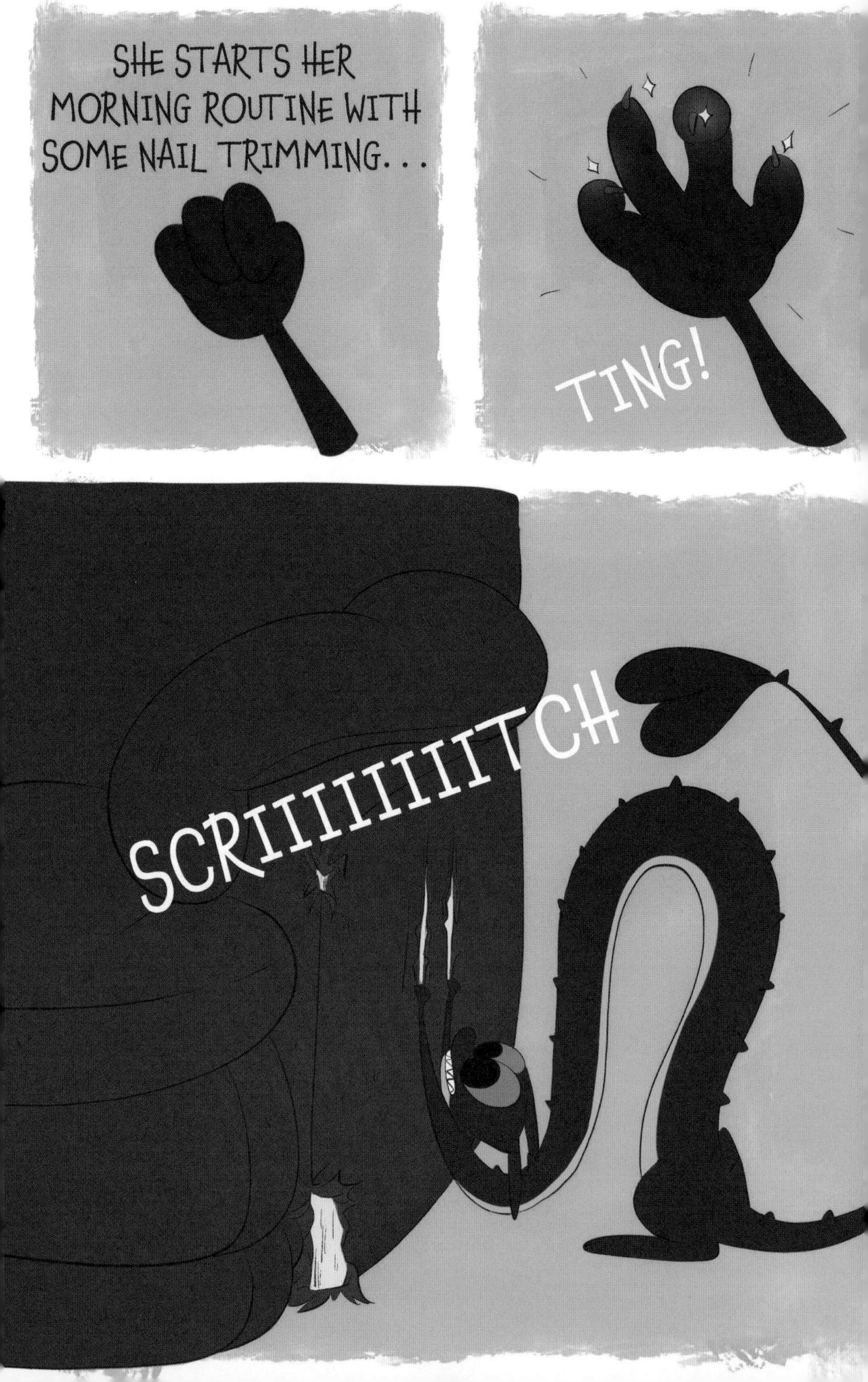
SHE STARTS HER MORNING ROUTINE WITH SOME NAIL TRIMMING...
TING!
SCRIIIIIIIITCH

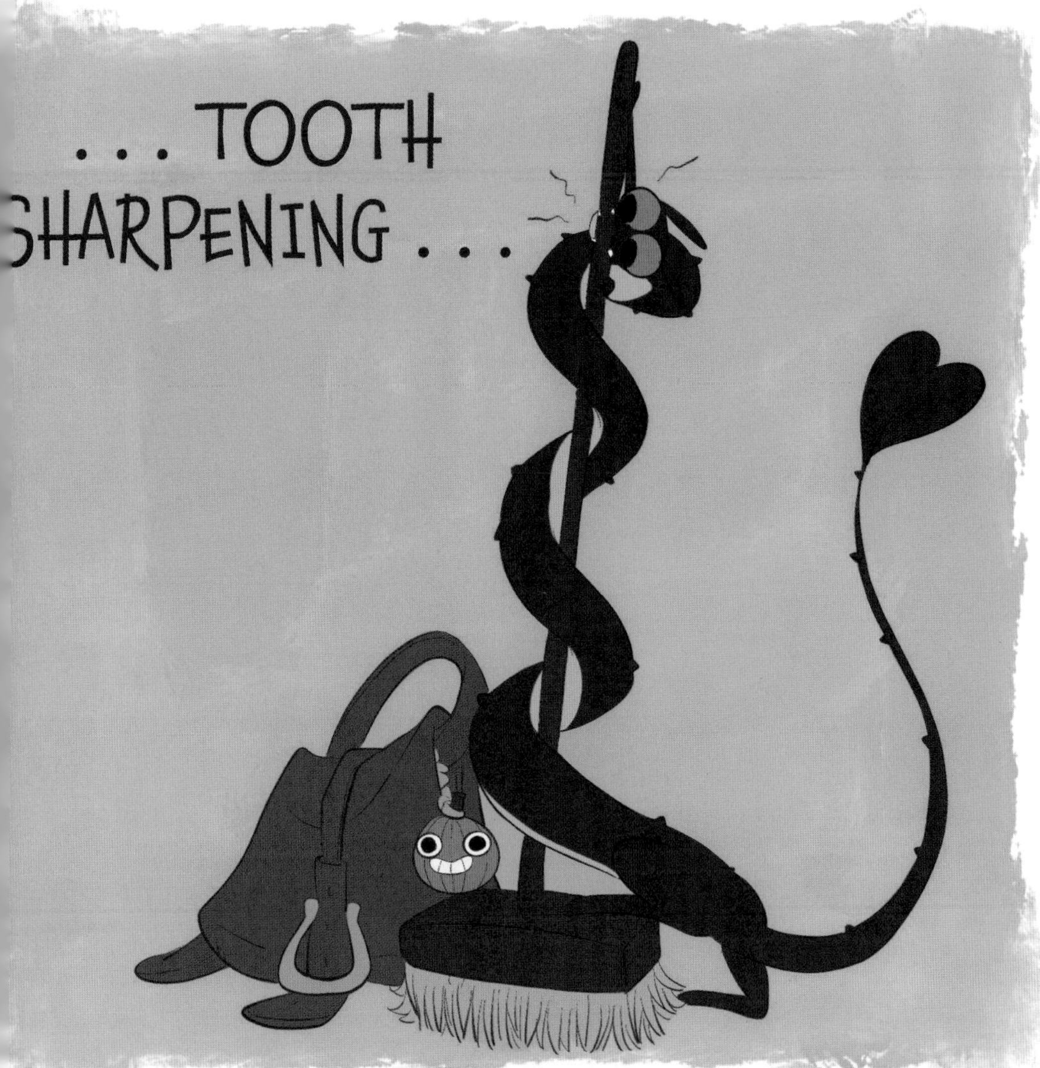
. . . TOOTH
SHARPENING . . .

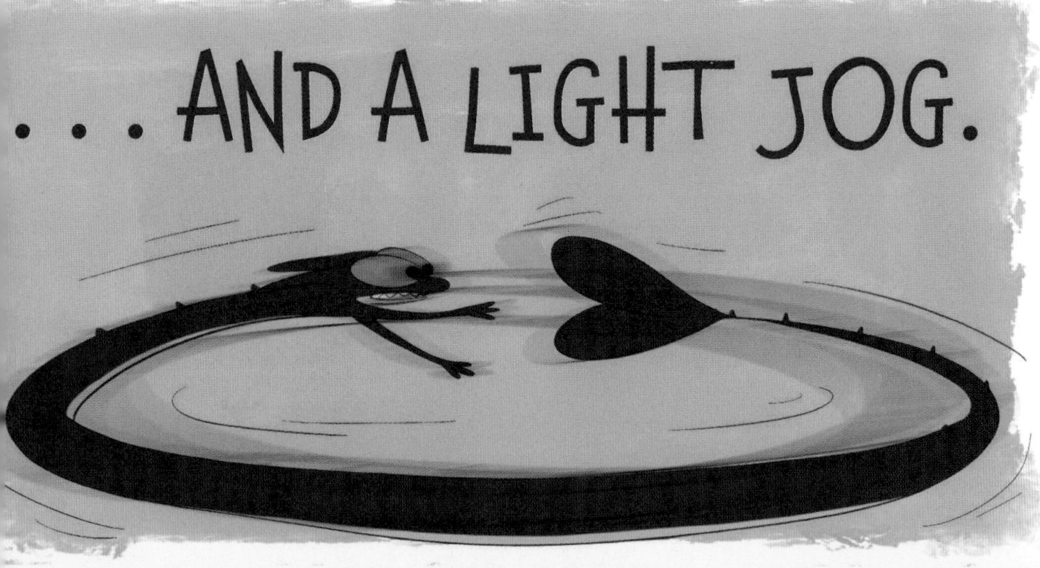
. . . AND A LIGHT JOG.

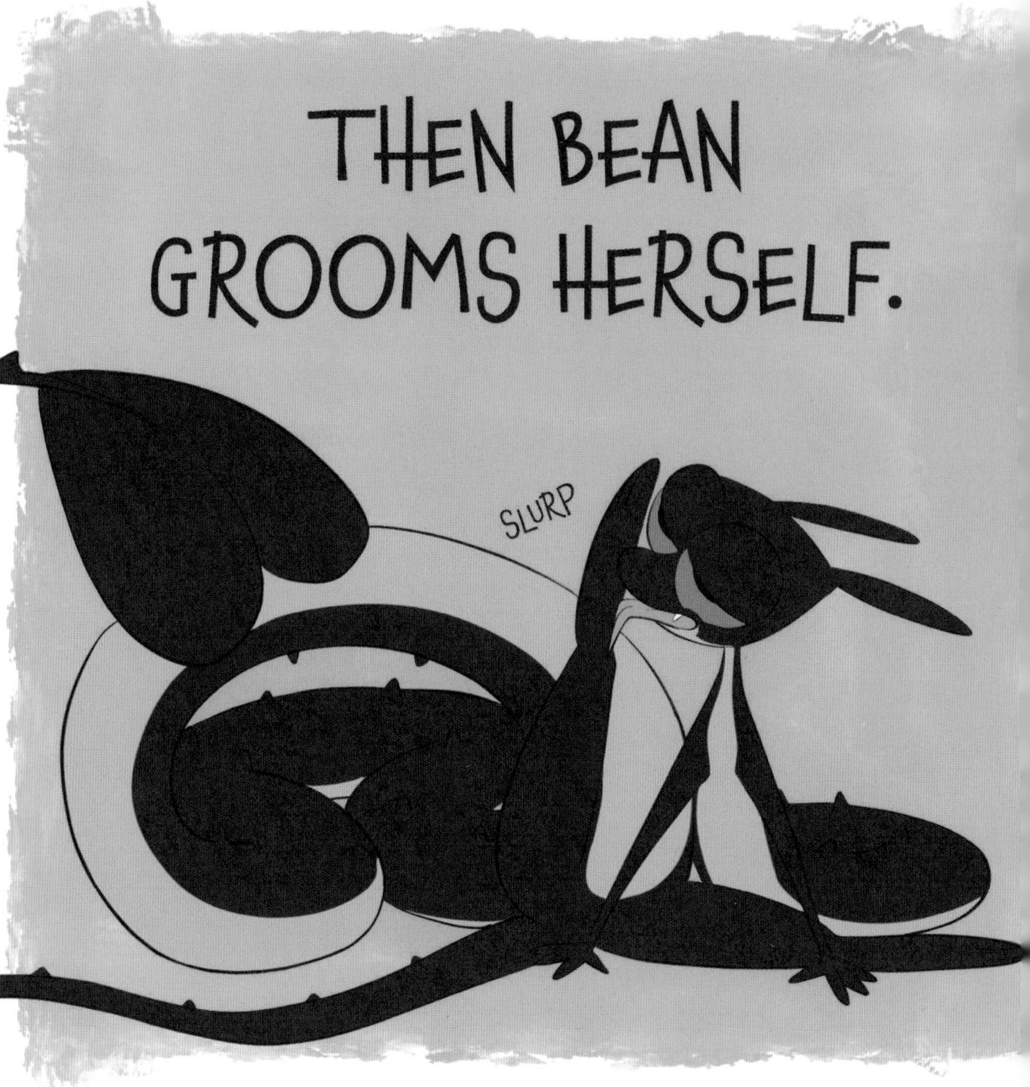
THEN BEAN
GROOMS HERSELF.
SLURP

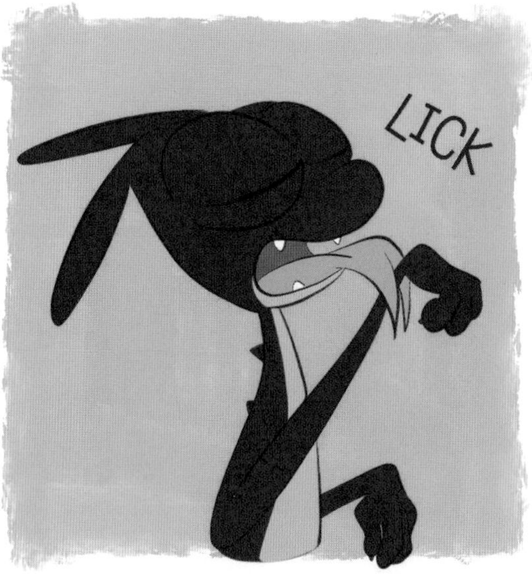
LICK

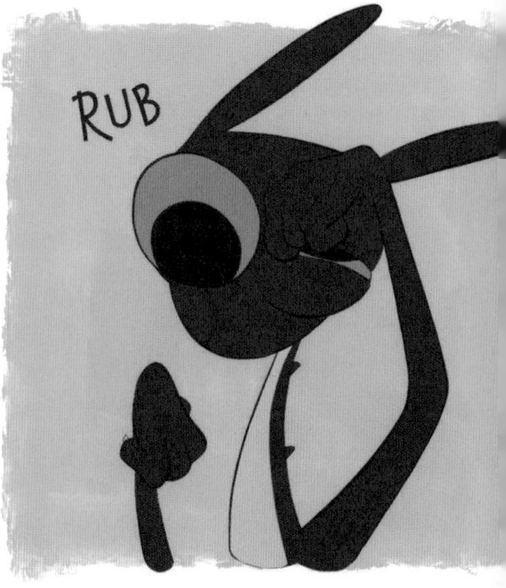
RUB

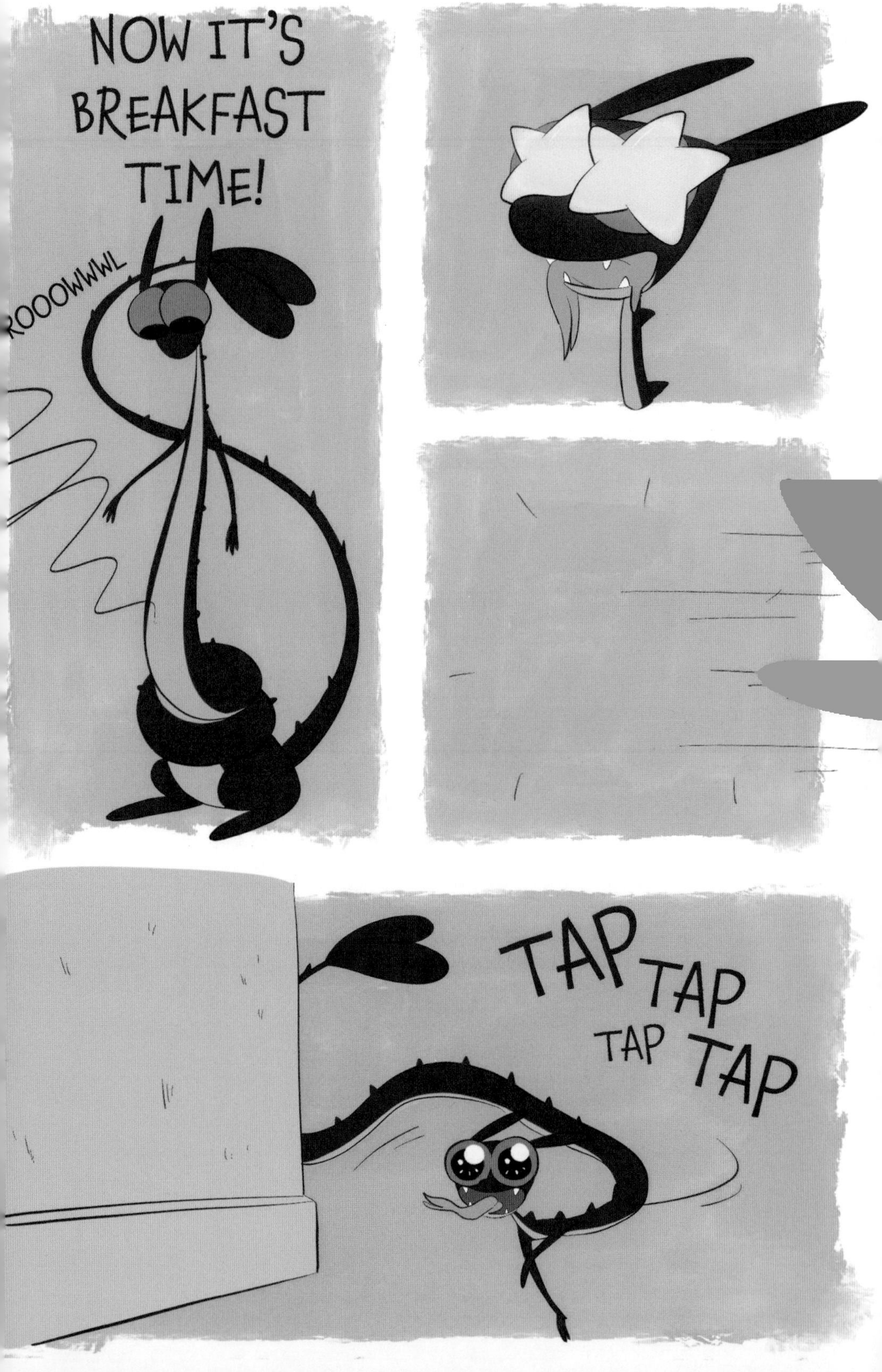
NOW IT'S BREAKFAST TIME!
ROOOWWWL
TAP TAP TAP TAP

BEAN'S FAVORITE MEAL

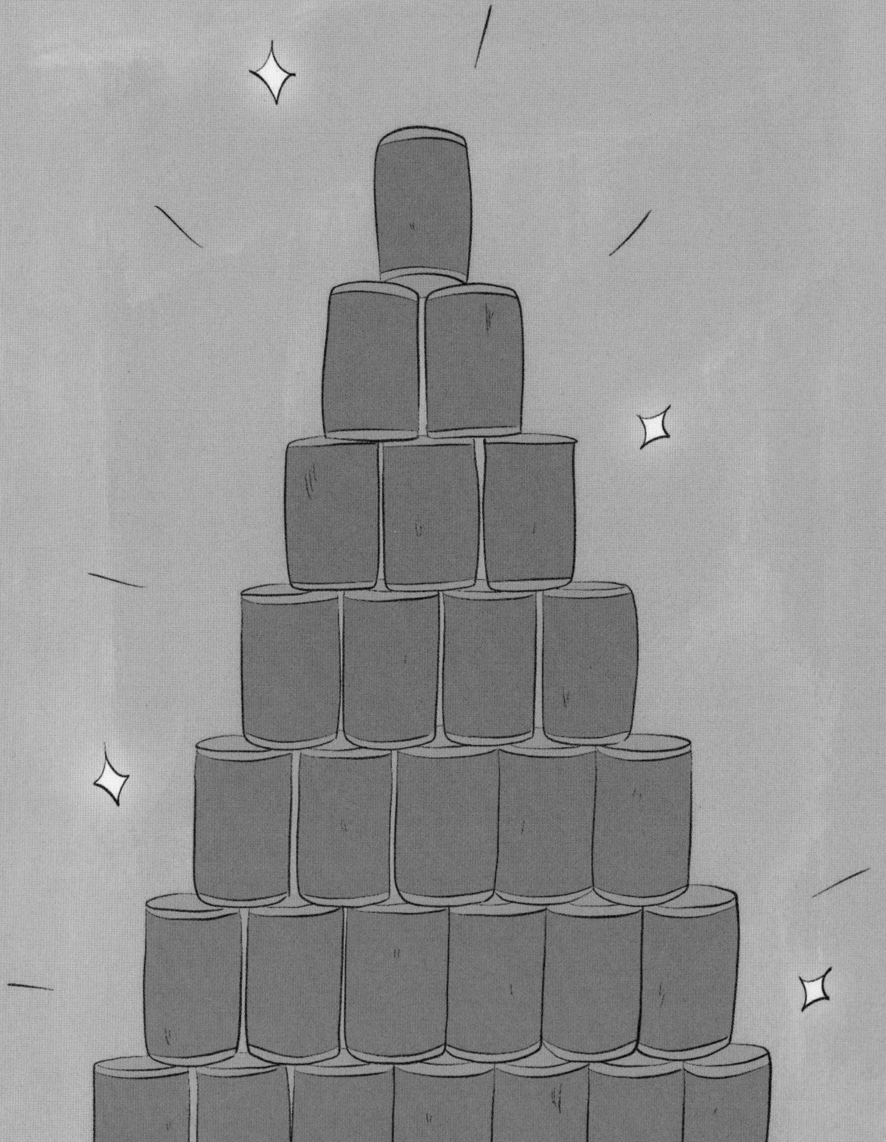

IS BEANS.

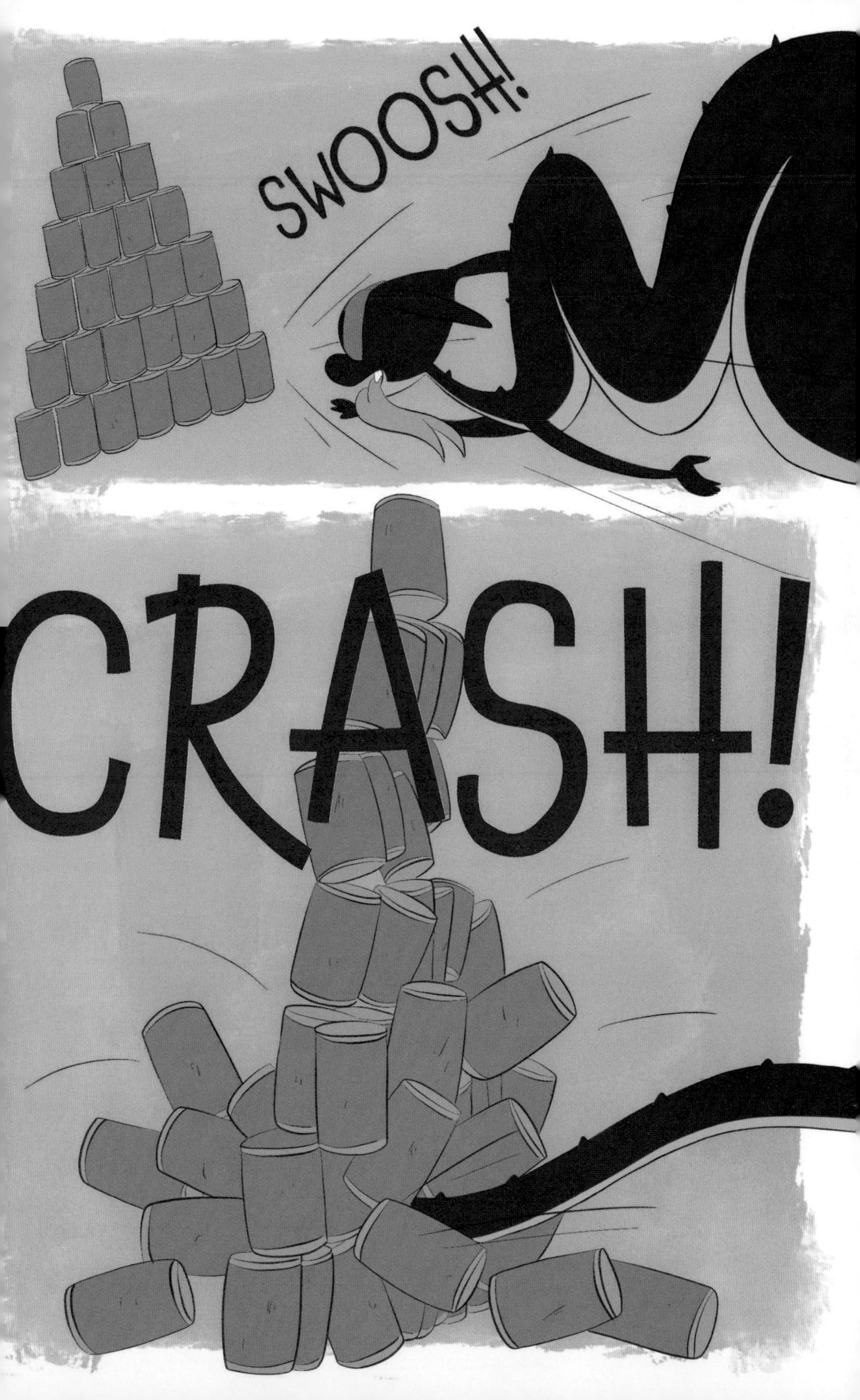
SWOOSH!
CRASH!

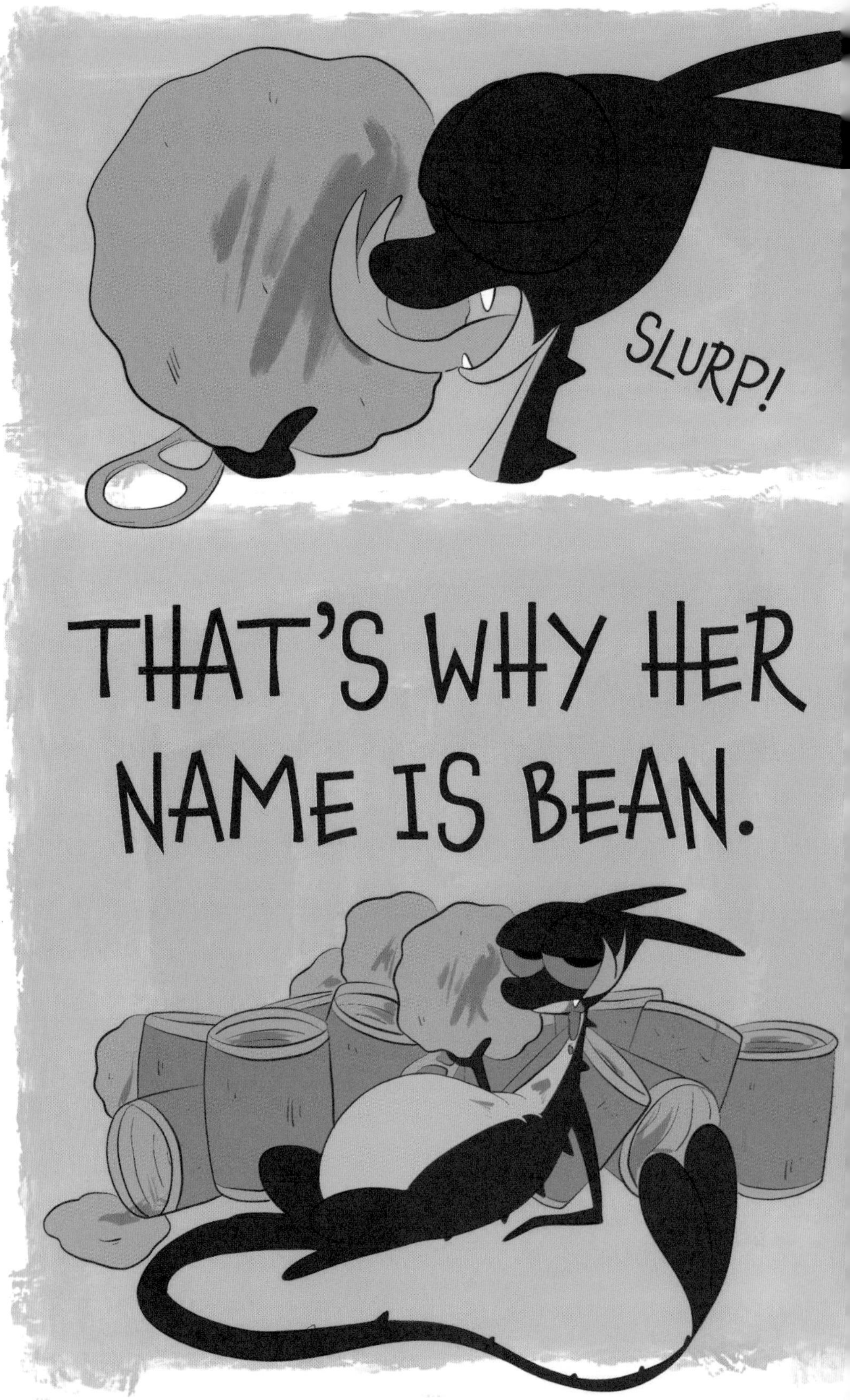
SLURP!
THAT'S WHY HER NAME IS BEAN.

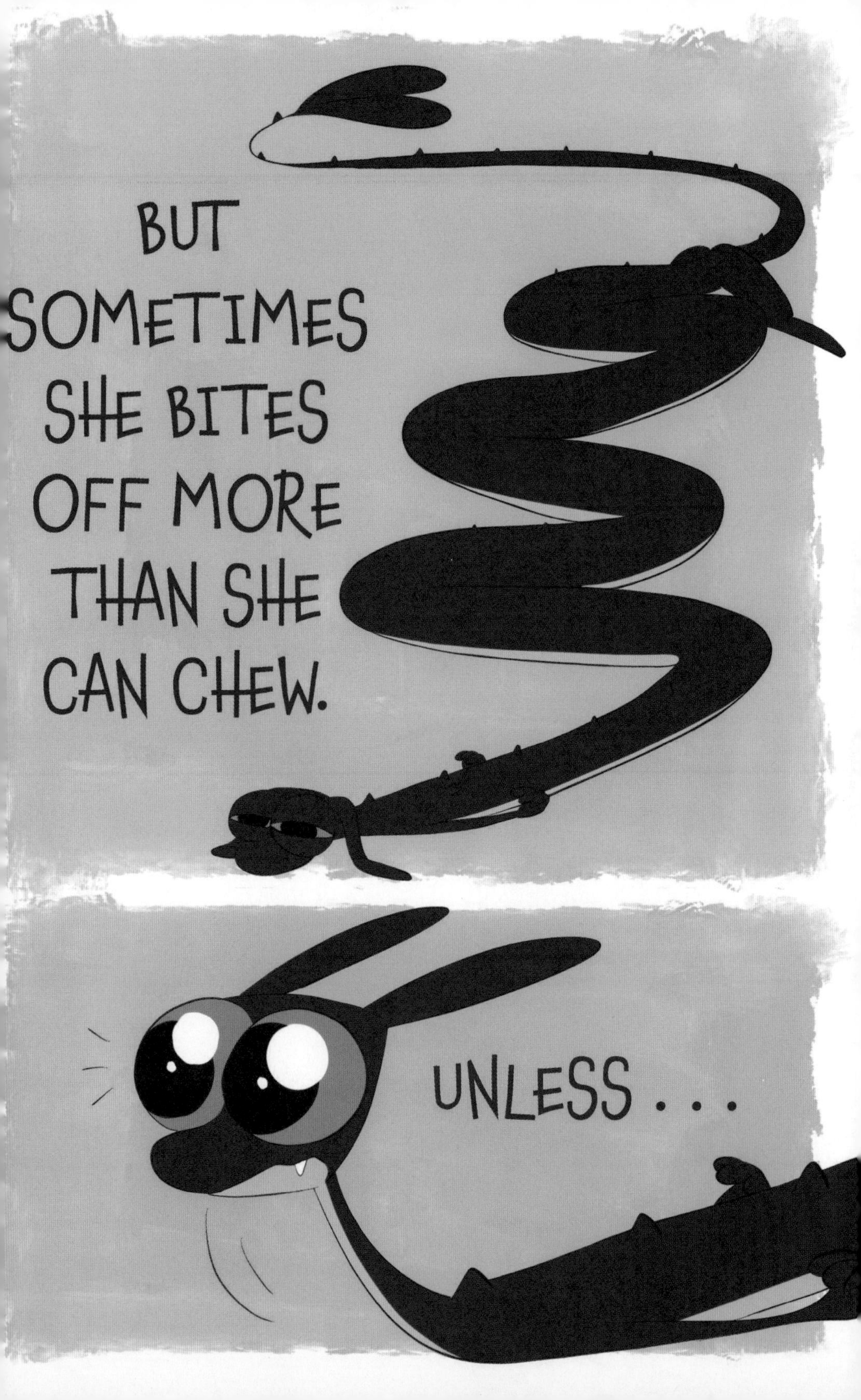
BUT SOMETIMES SHE BITES OFF MORE THAN SHE CAN CHEW.
UNLESS . . .

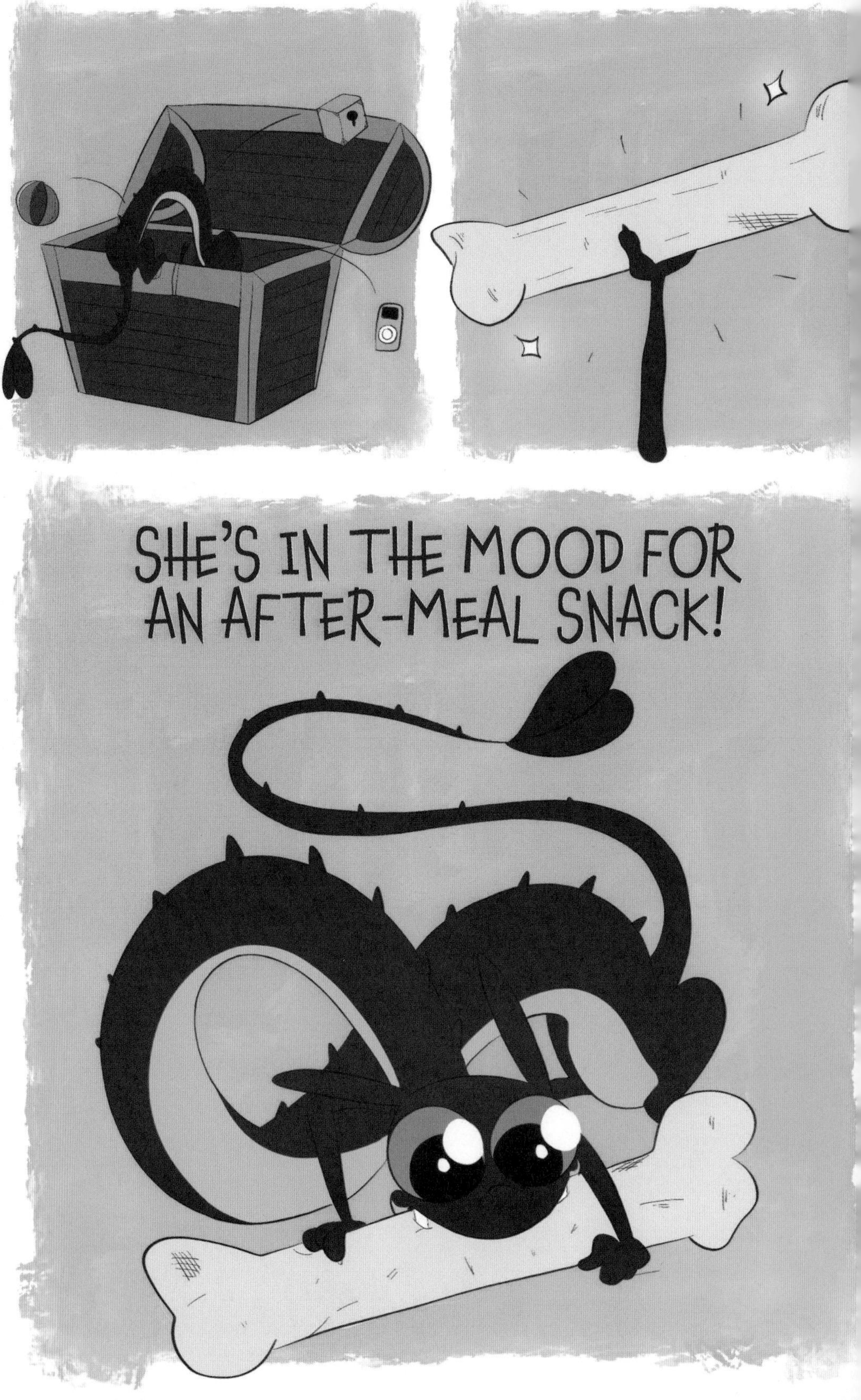
SHE'S IN THE MOOD FOR AN AFTER-MEAL SNACK!

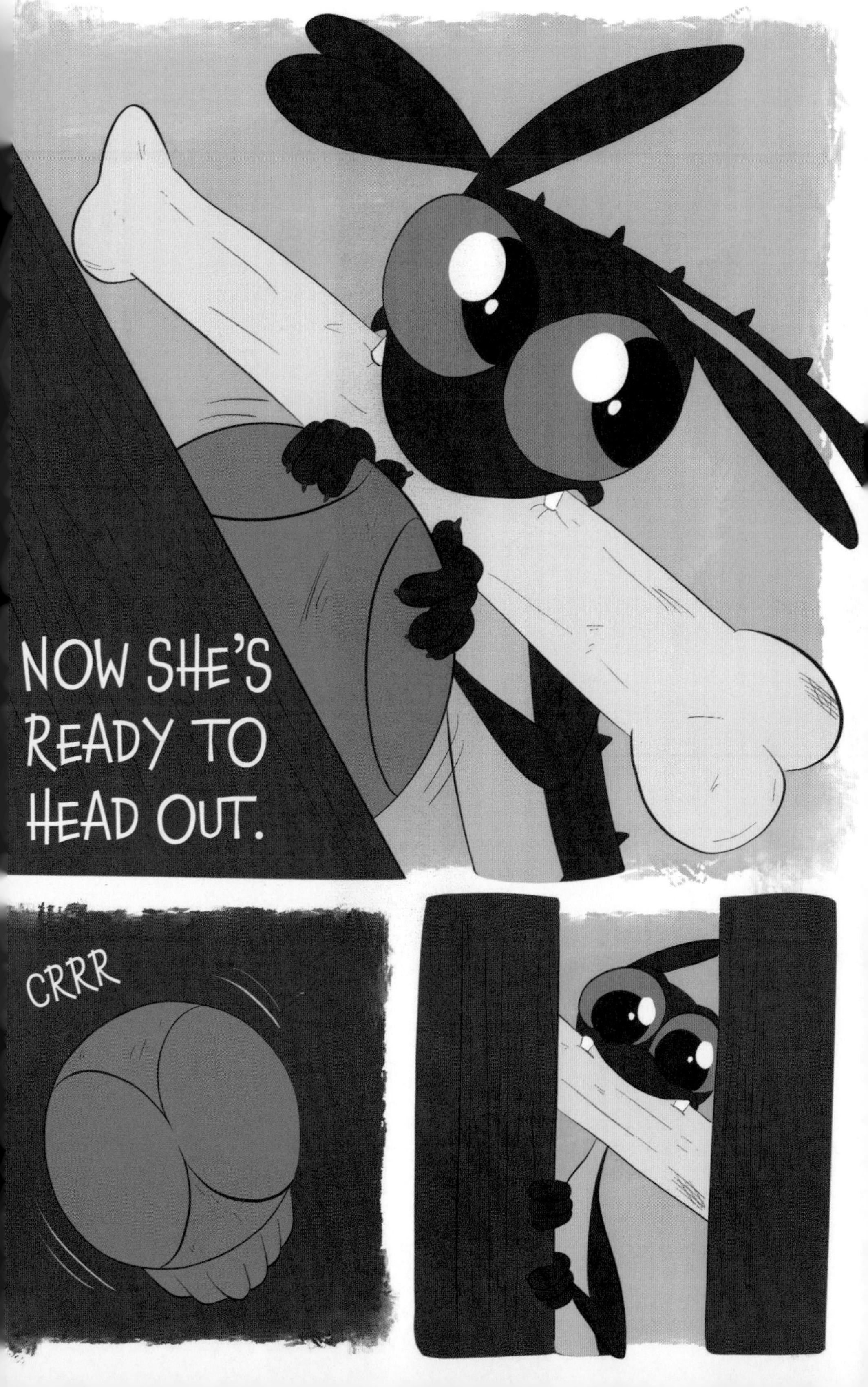
NOW SHE'S READY TO HEAD OUT.
CRRR

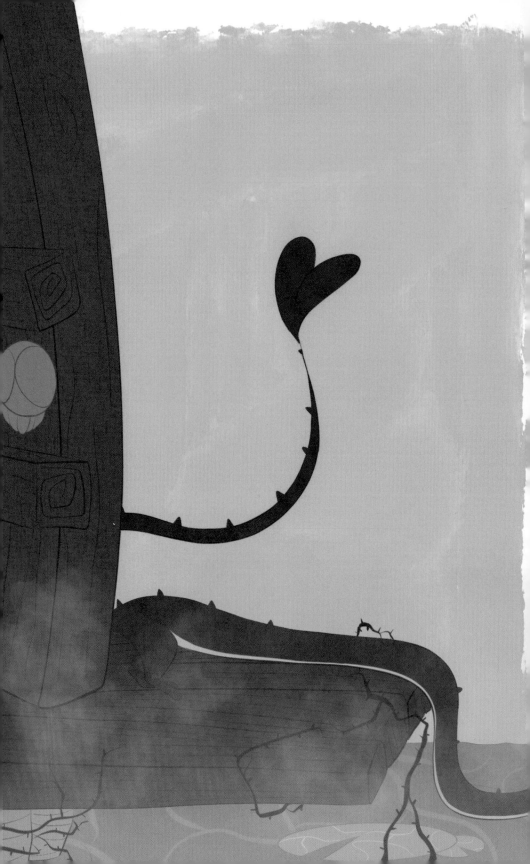

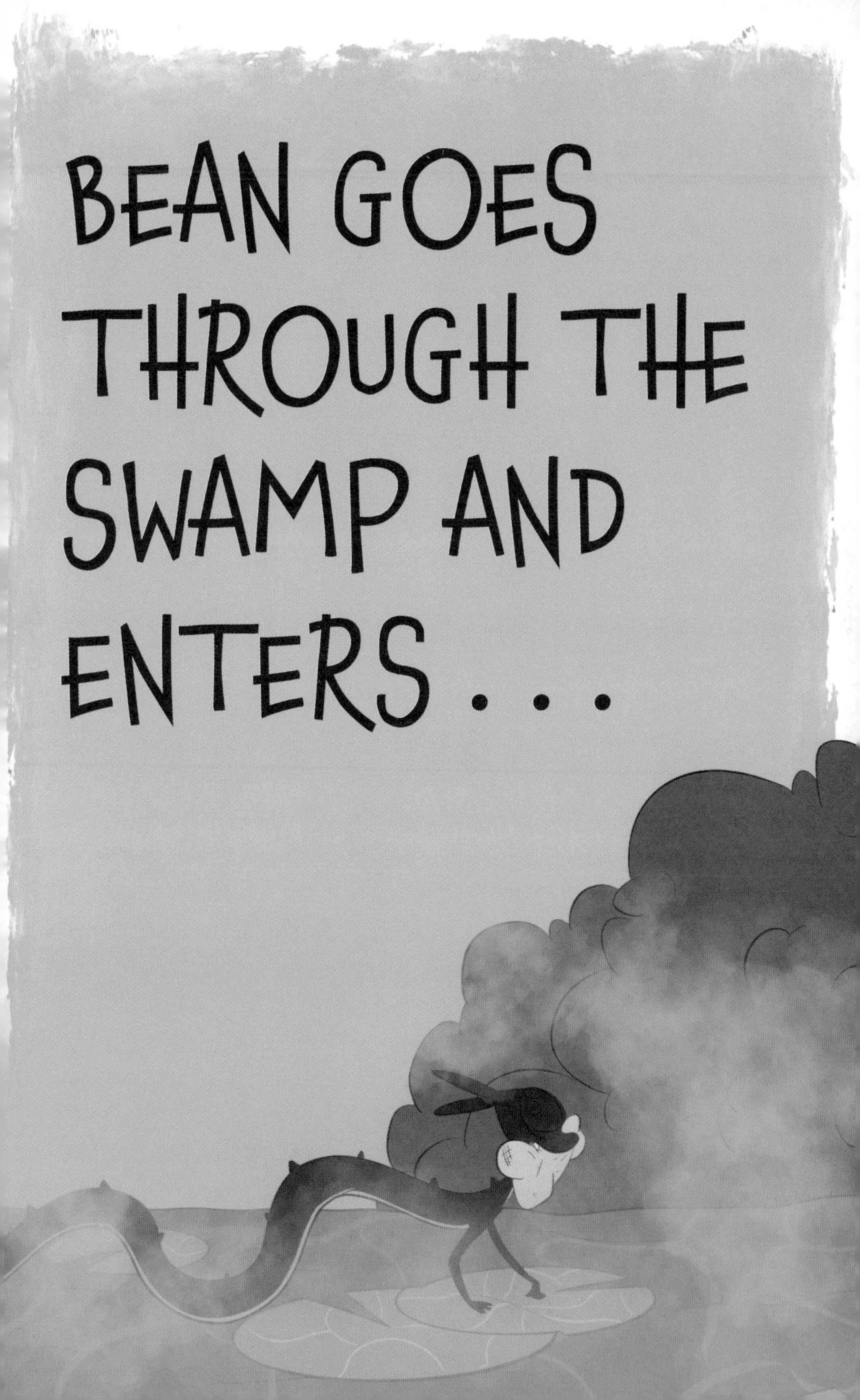
BEAN GOES THROUGH THE SWAMP AND ENTERS . . .

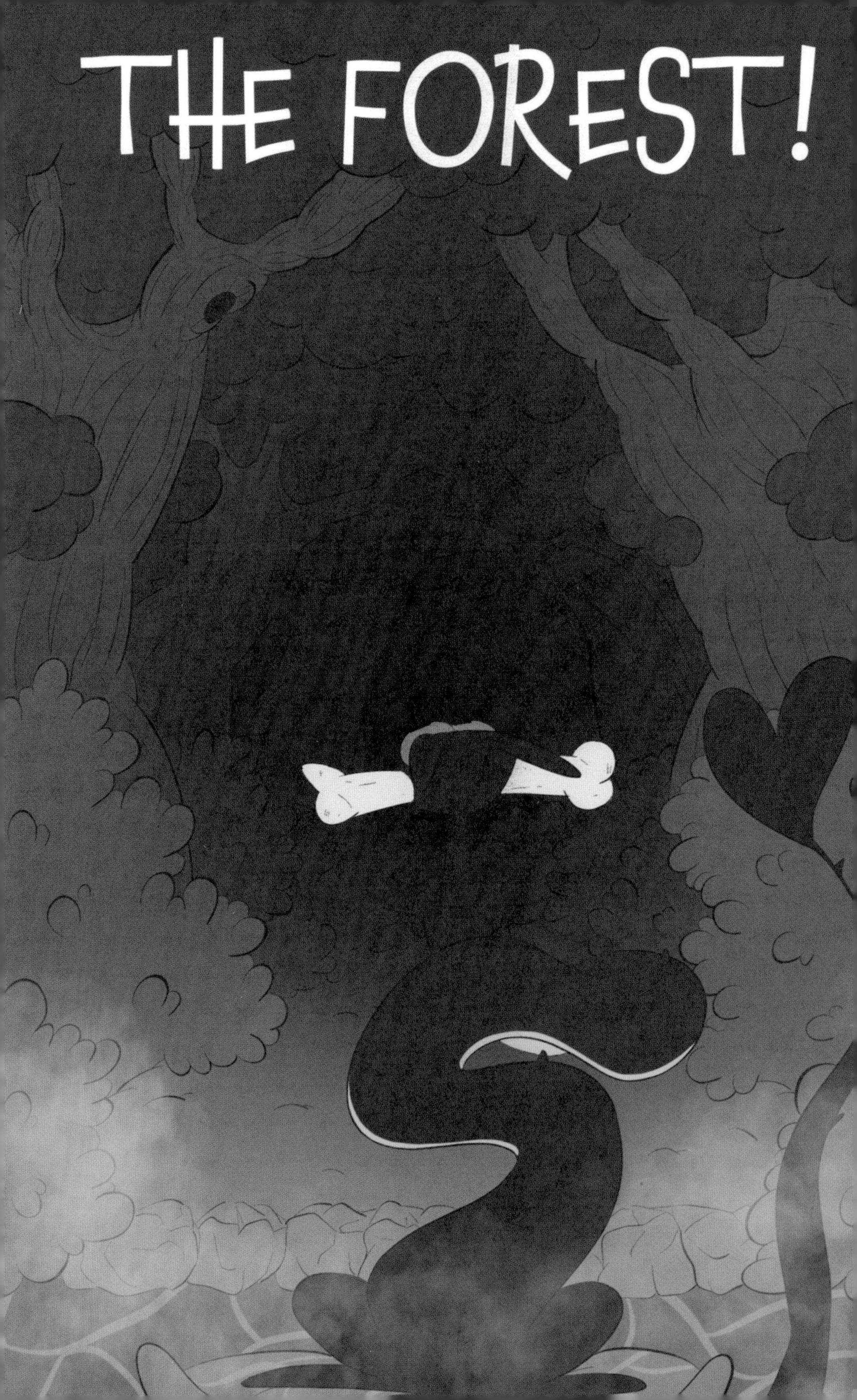
THE FOREST!

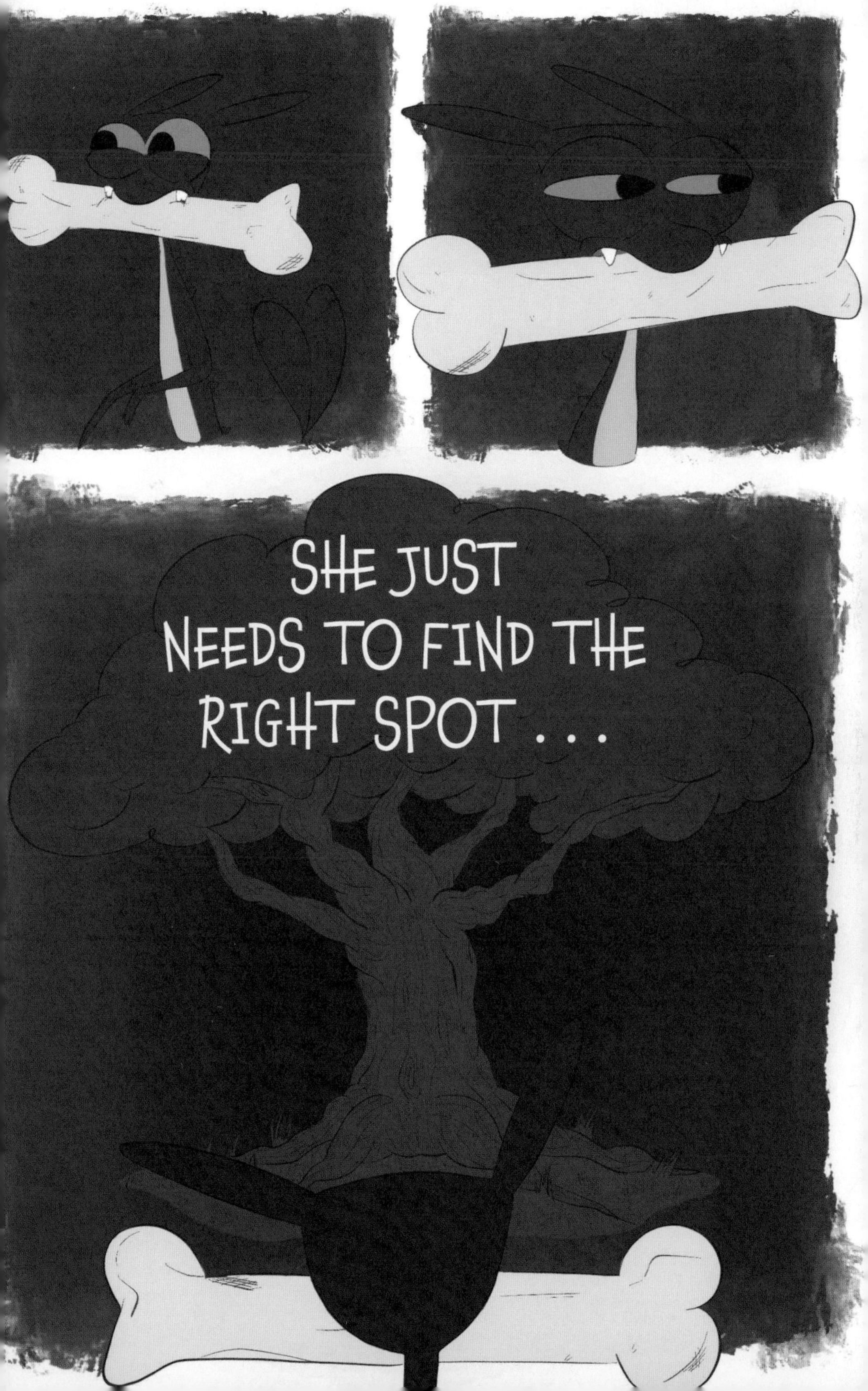
SHE JUST NEEDS TO FIND THE RIGHT SPOT . . .

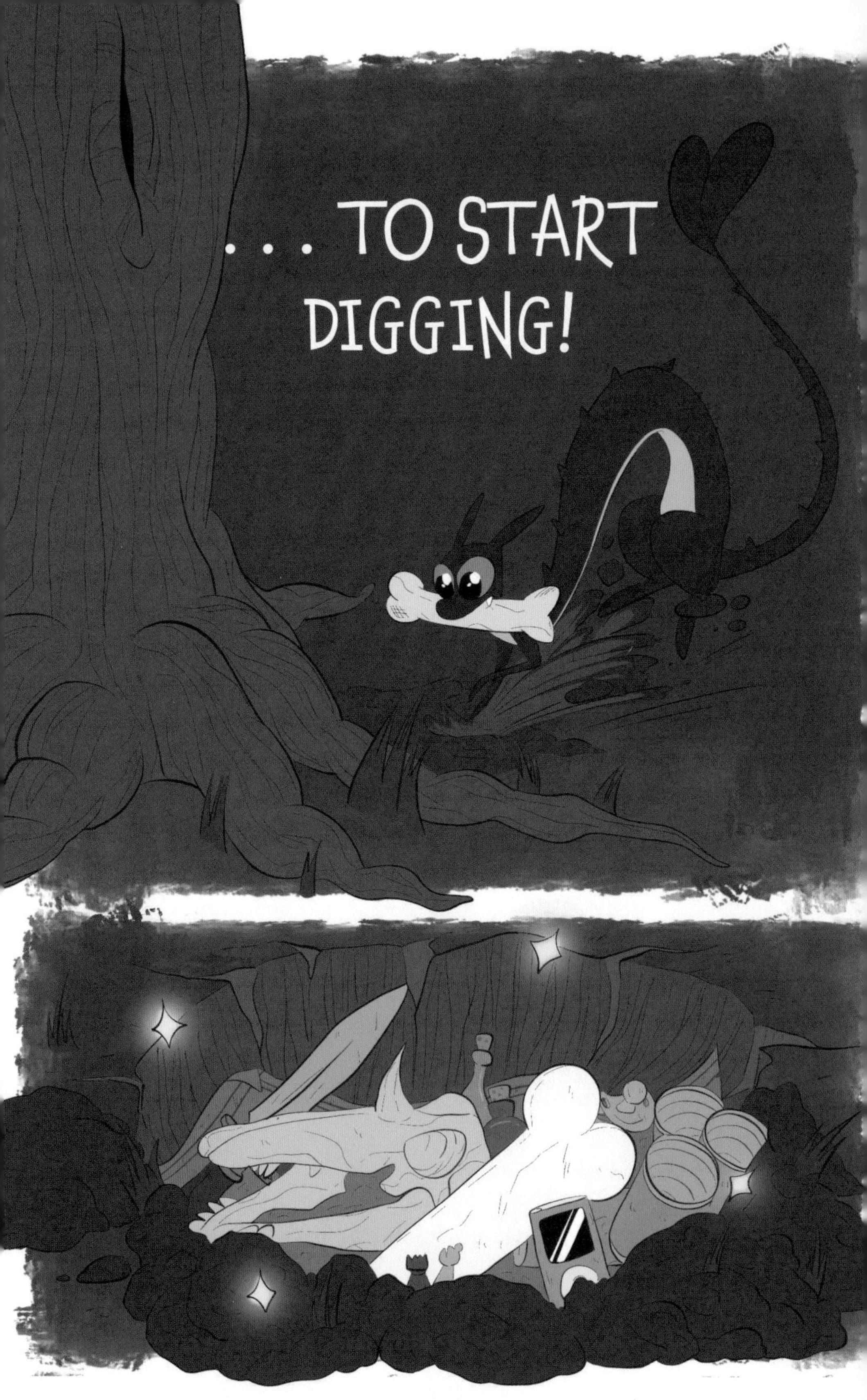
. . . TO START DIGGING!

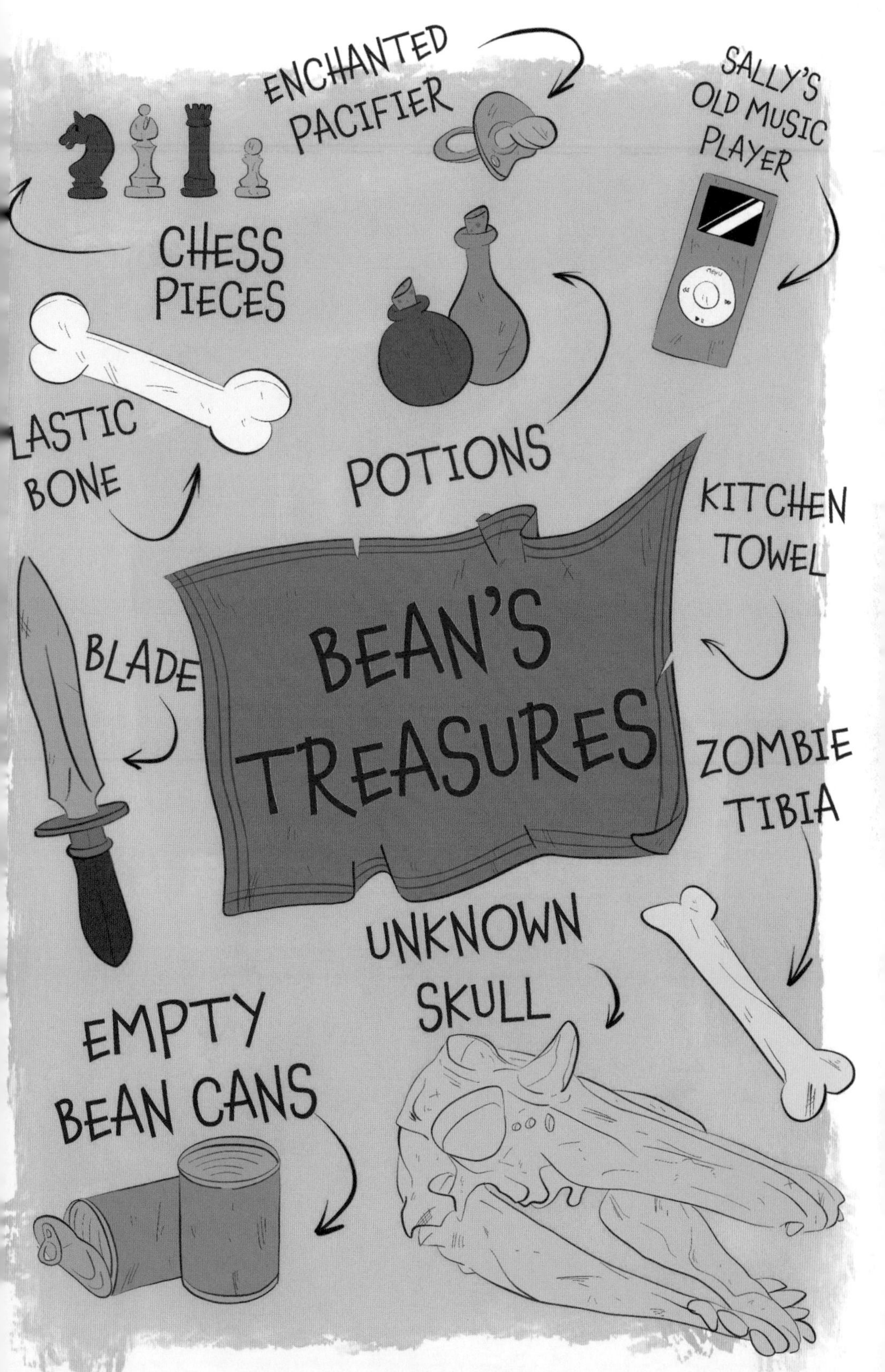
BEAN'S TREASURES
CHESS PIECES
ENCHANTED PACIFIER
SALLY'S OLD MUSIC PLAYER
LASTIC BONE
POTIONS
KITCHEN TOWEL
BLADE
ZOMBIE TIBIA
UNKNOWN SKULL
EMPTY BEAN CANS

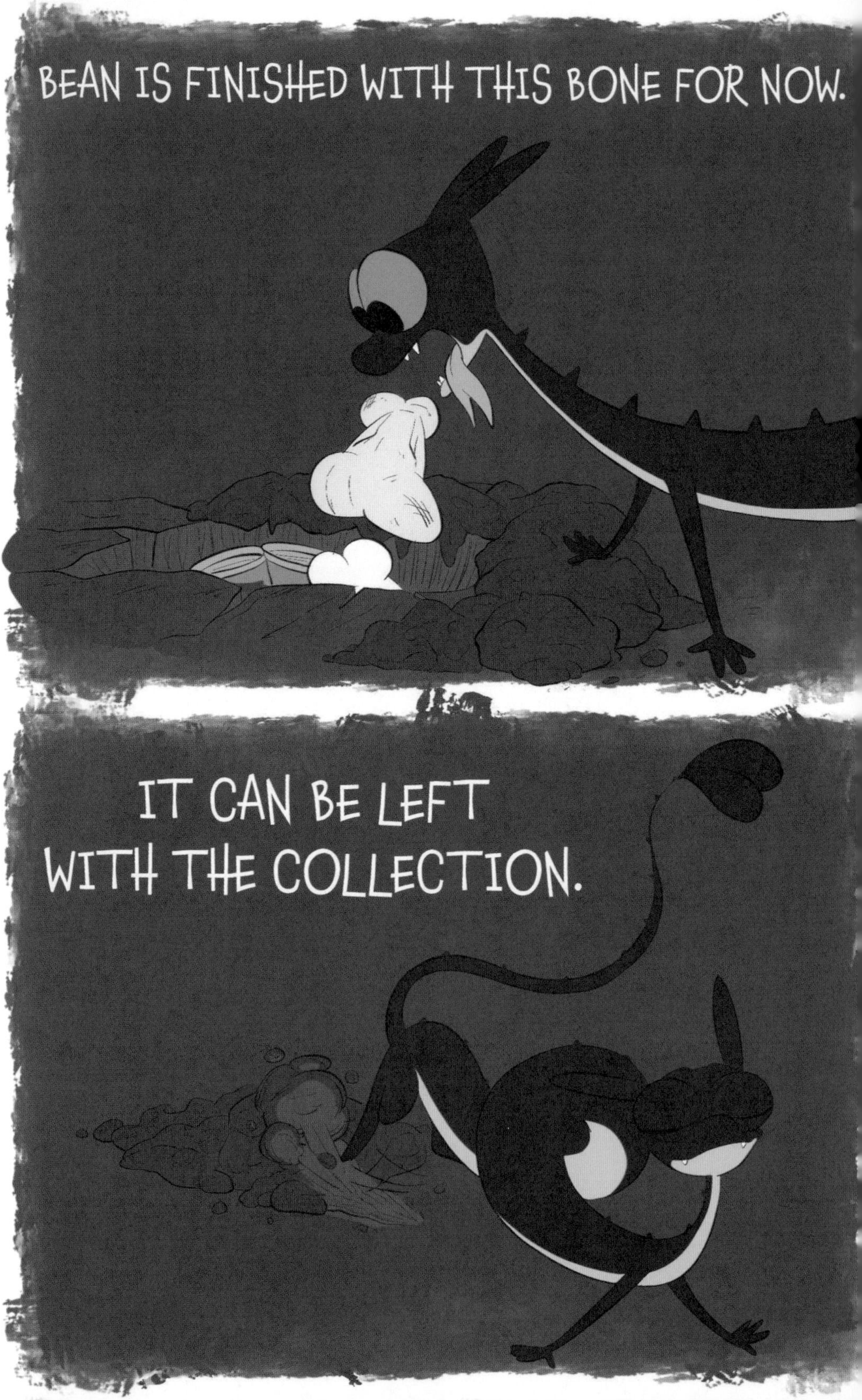
BEAN IS FINISHED WITH THIS BONE FOR NOW.
IT CAN BE LEFT WITH THE COLLECTION.

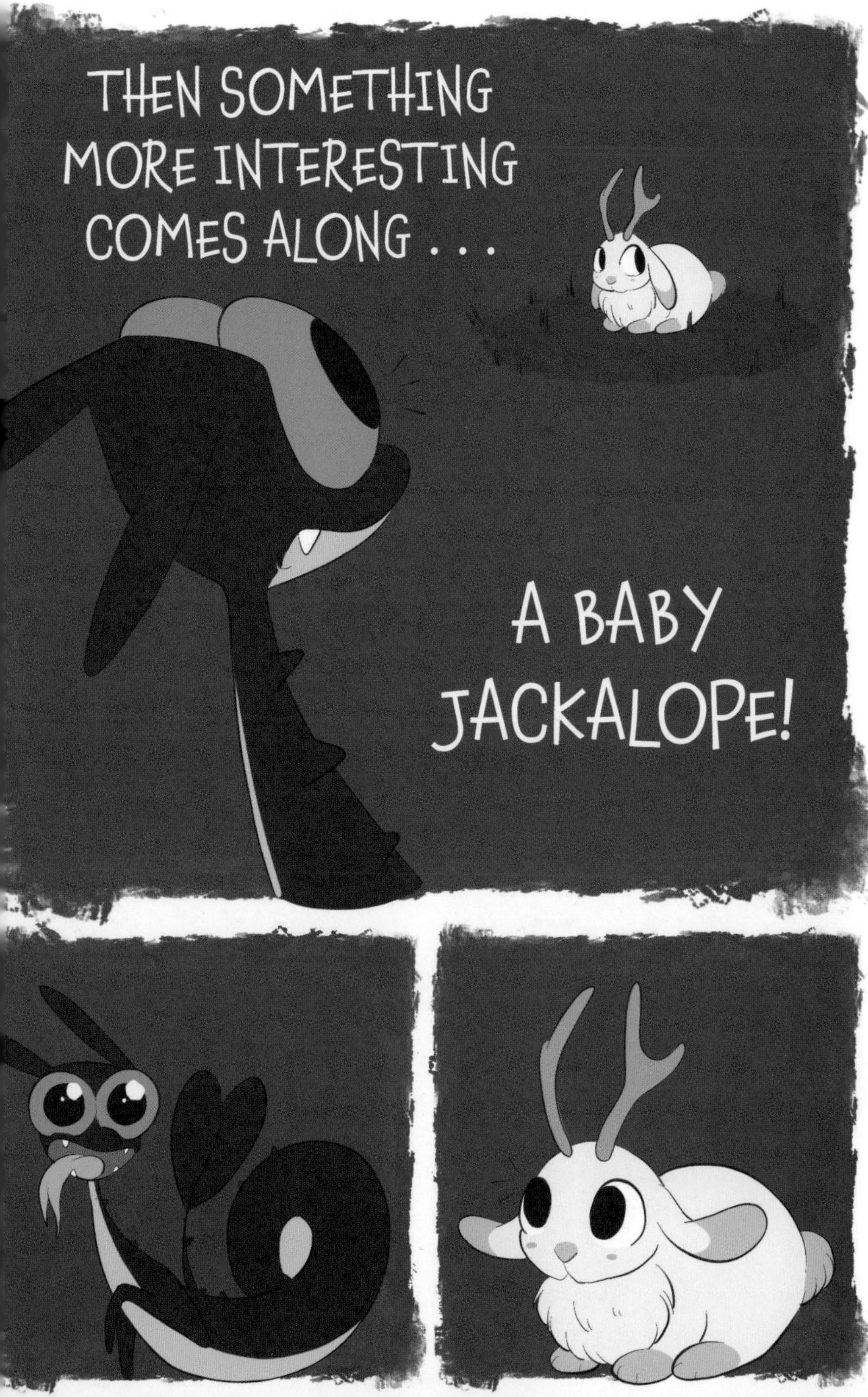
THEN SOMETHING MORE INTERESTING COMES ALONG . . .
A BABY JACKALOPE!

BEAN LOVES TO CHASE THEM.

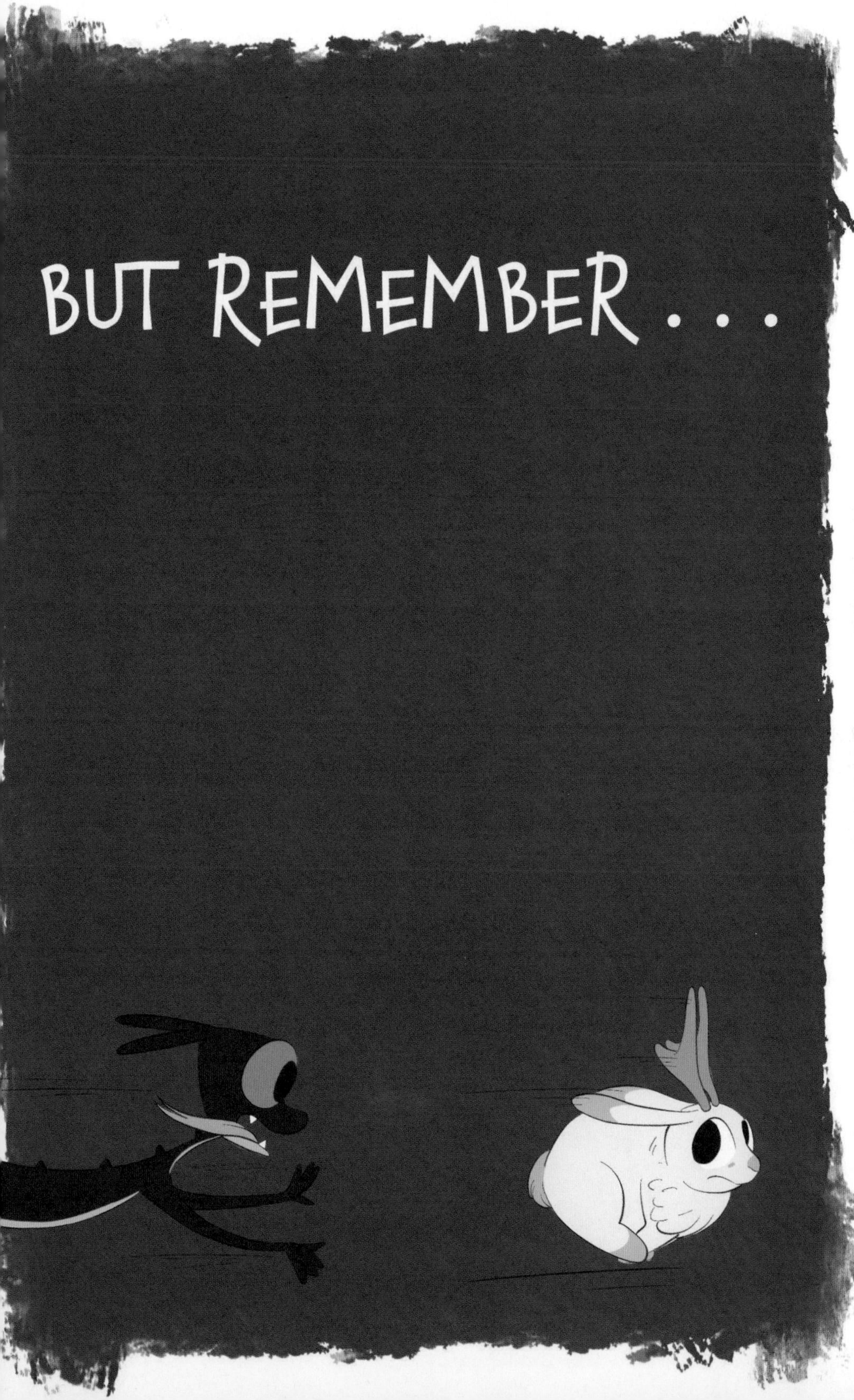
BUT REMEMBER . . .

THE MOM
IS NEVER FAR!

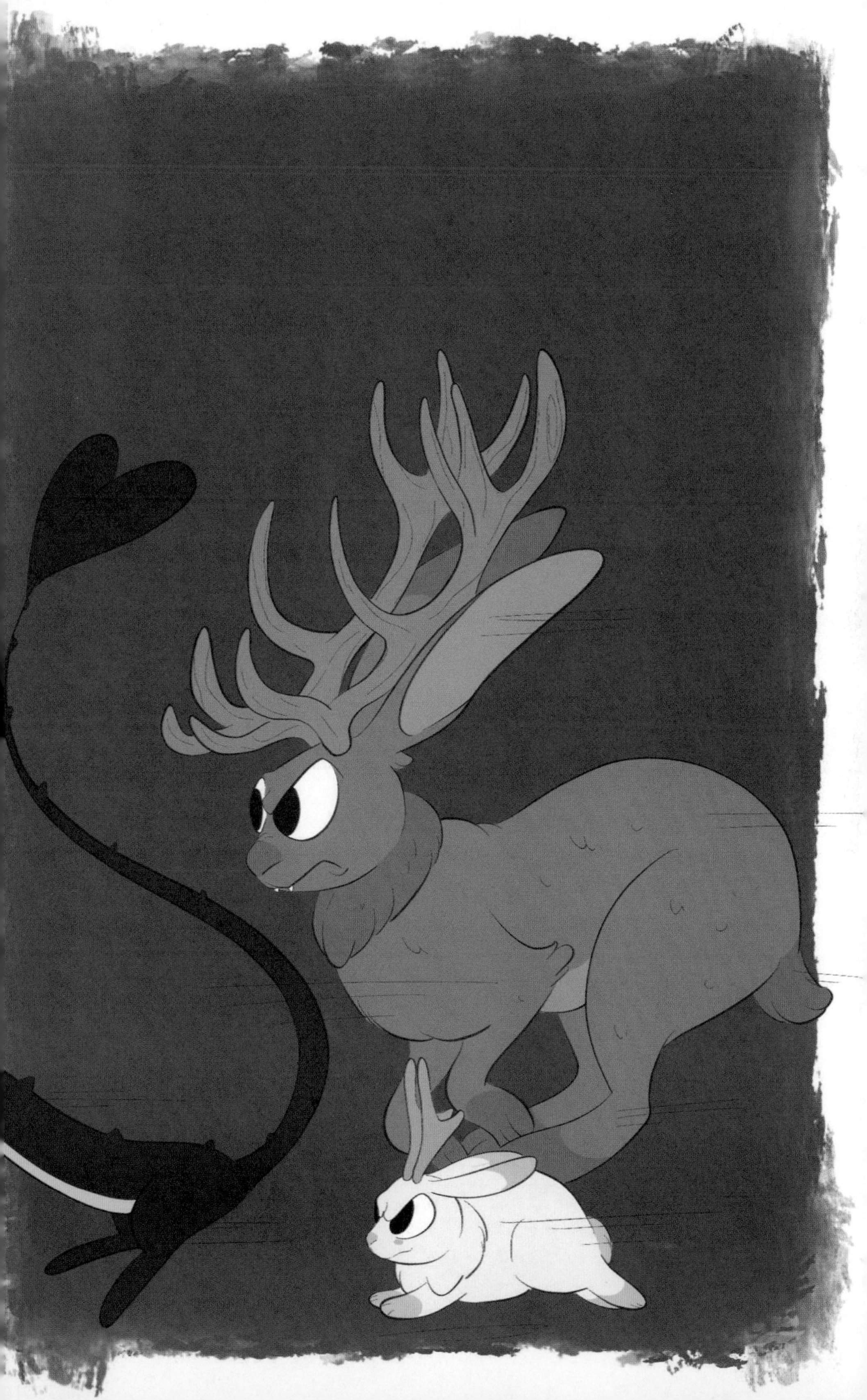

THE JACKALOPE

Half jackrabbit, half antelope, the Jackalope is a fearsome critter that can run at incredible speed and mimic the human voice. Sadly, they are hunted down for their antlers, which behold powerful magic.

ANTLERS

FANGS

CUTE TAIL

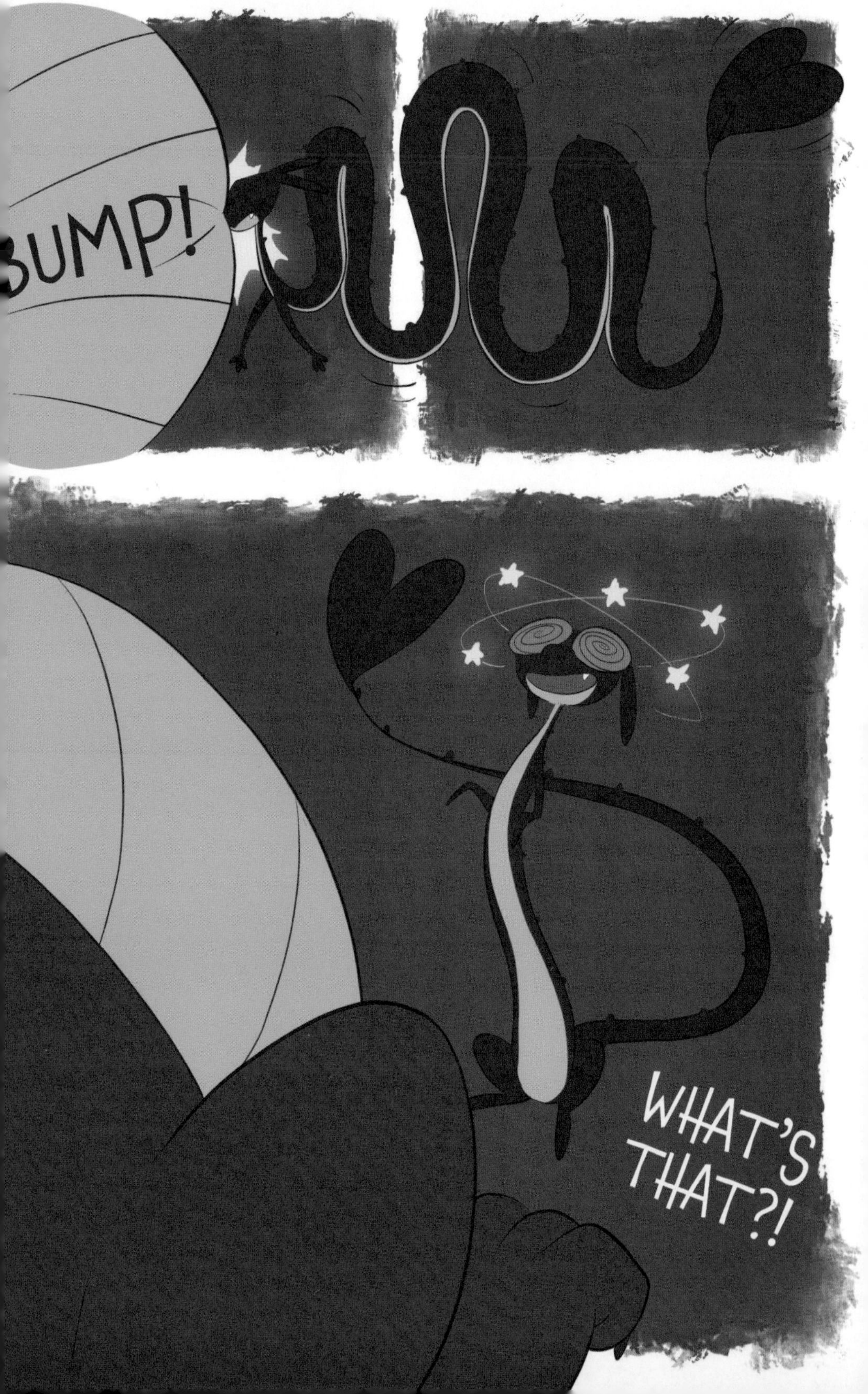
BUMP!
WHAT'S THAT?!

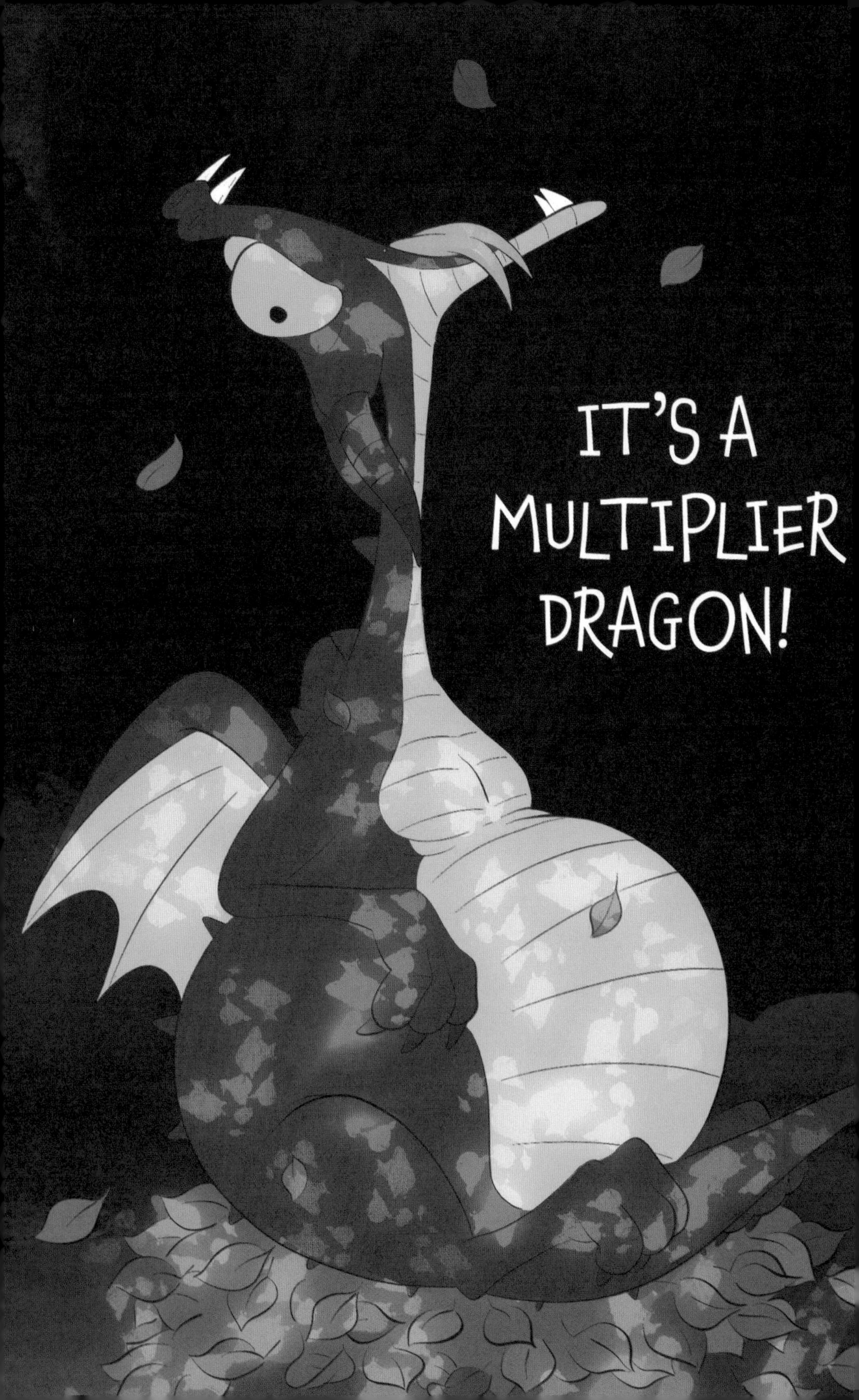
IT'S A
MULTIPLIER
DRAGON!

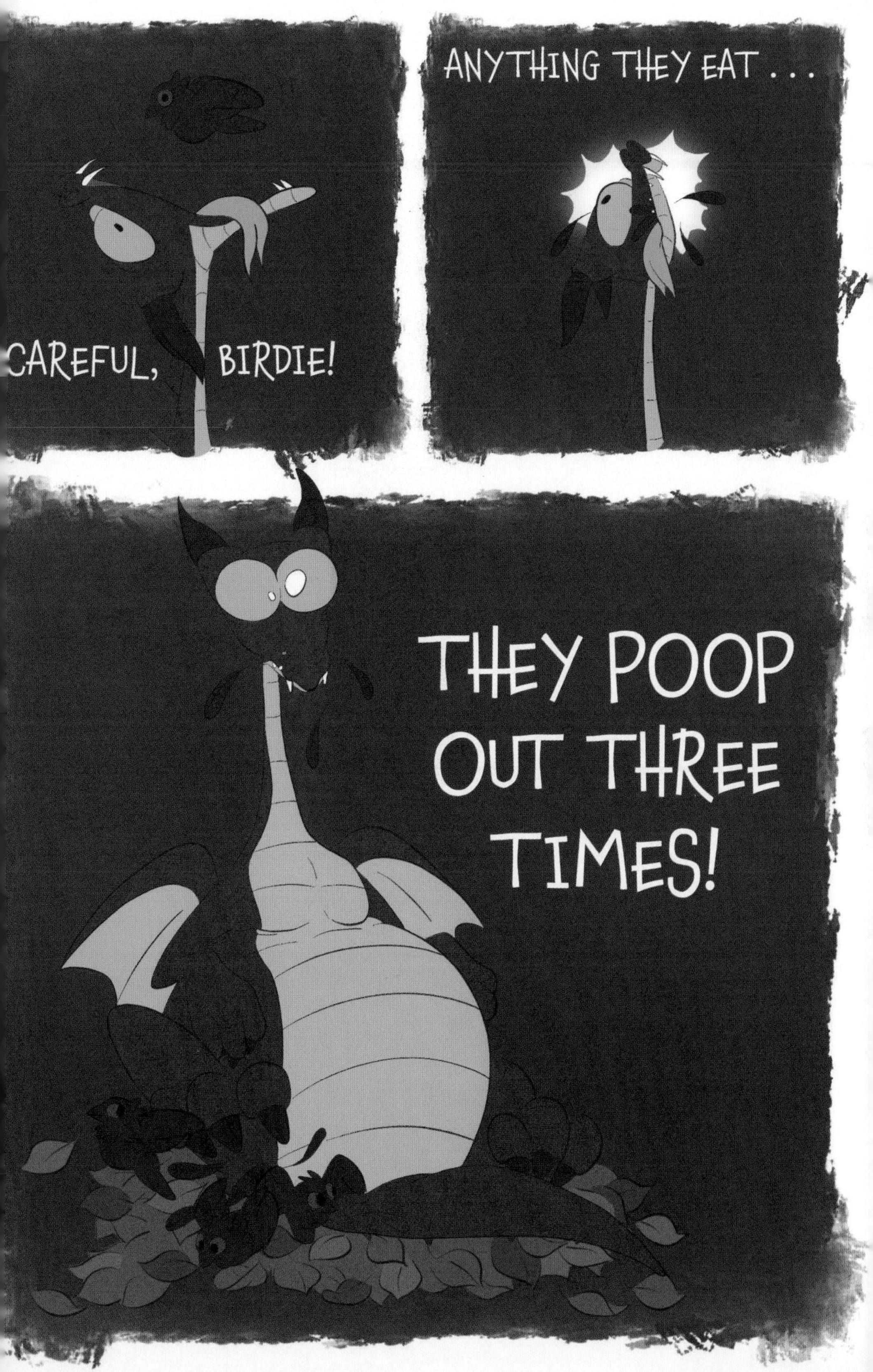
CAREFUL, BIRDIE!
ANYTHING THEY EAT . . .
THEY POOP OUT THREE TIMES!

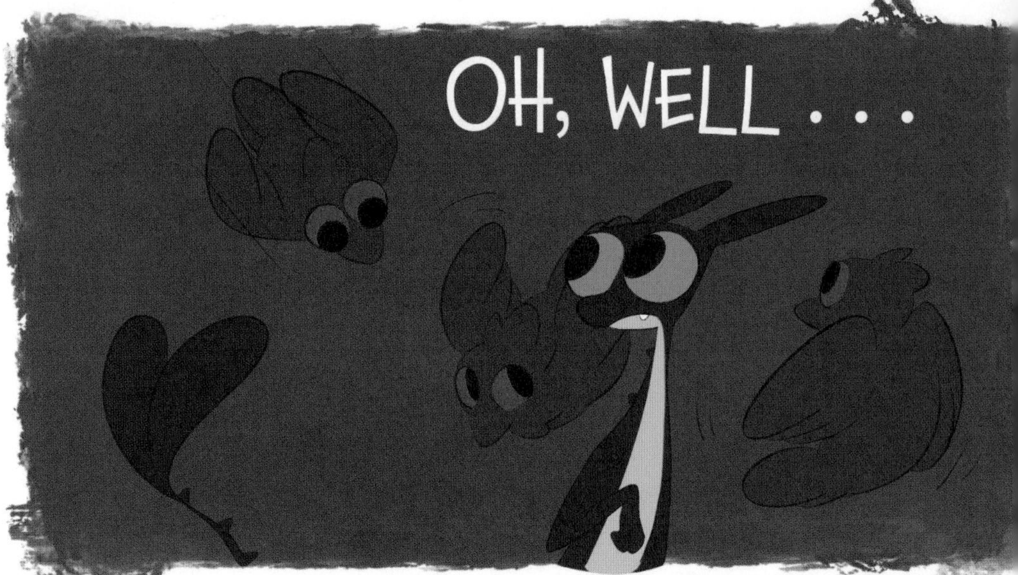
OH, WELL . . .

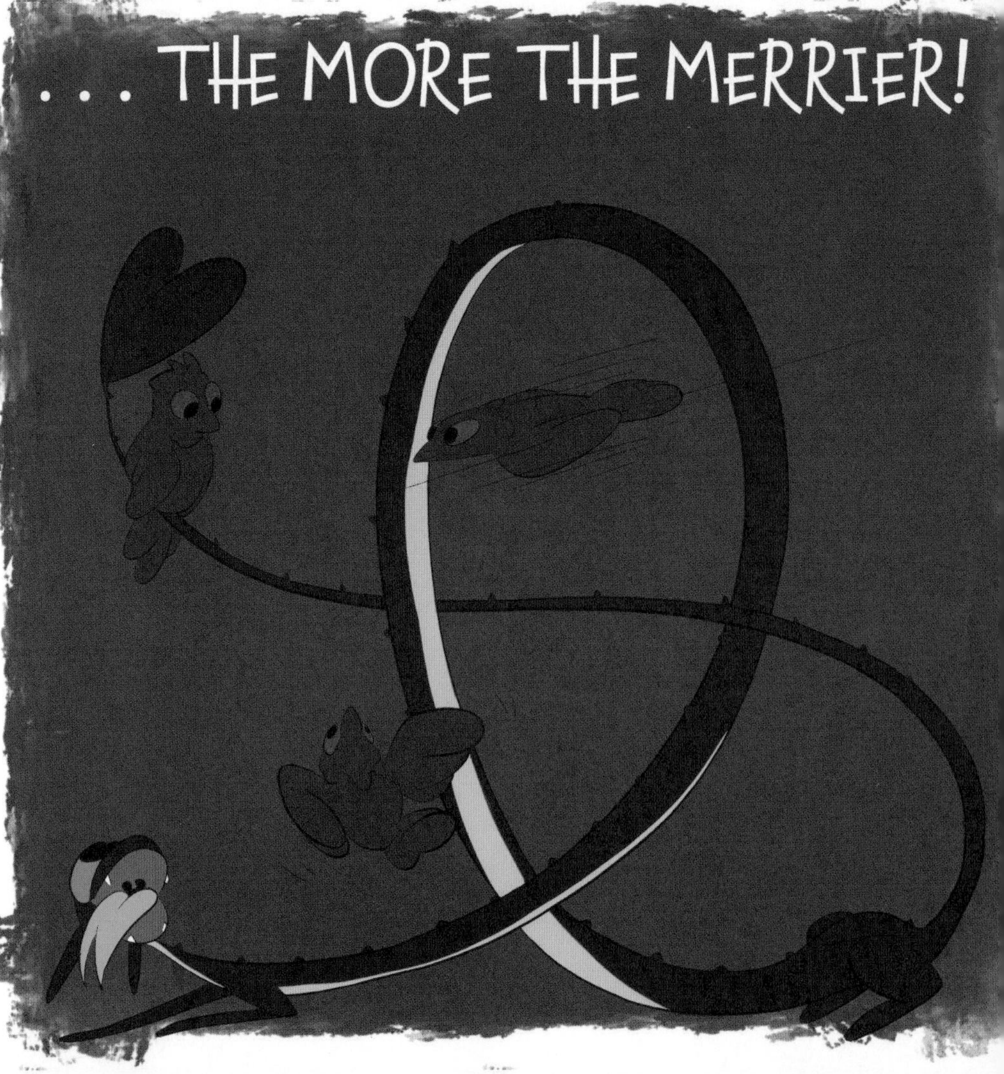
. . . THE MORE THE MERRIER!

THE MULTIPLIER

Multiplier dragons typically live secluded and alone on piles of whatever gets trapped in their open mouth.
They multiply everything they eat . . . except for gold!
They are often on the run from people looking to triple gems and jewels . . .

TILTING JAW

FULL BELLY

TREASURE

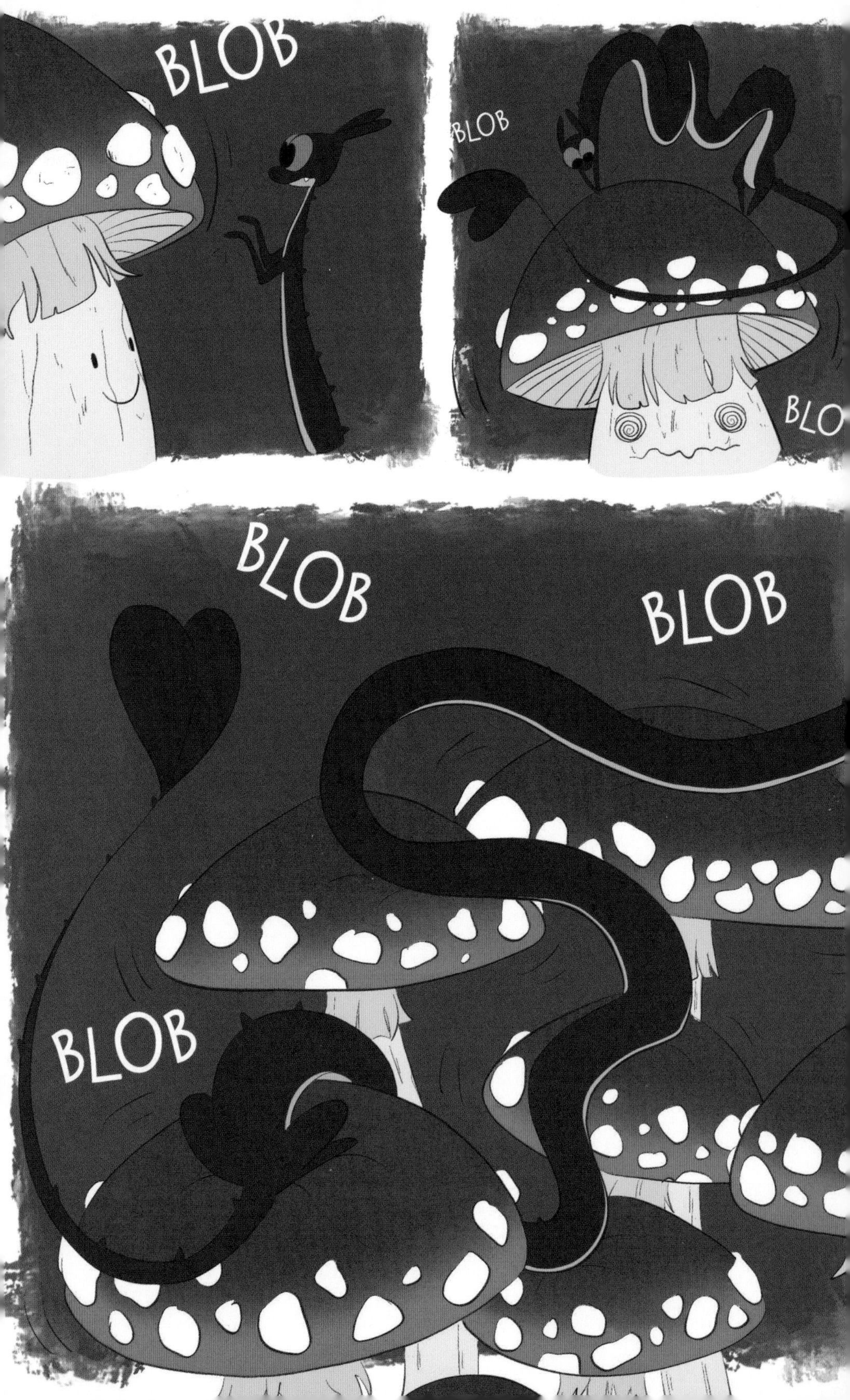

BLOB
BLOB
BLO
BLOB
BLOB
BLOB

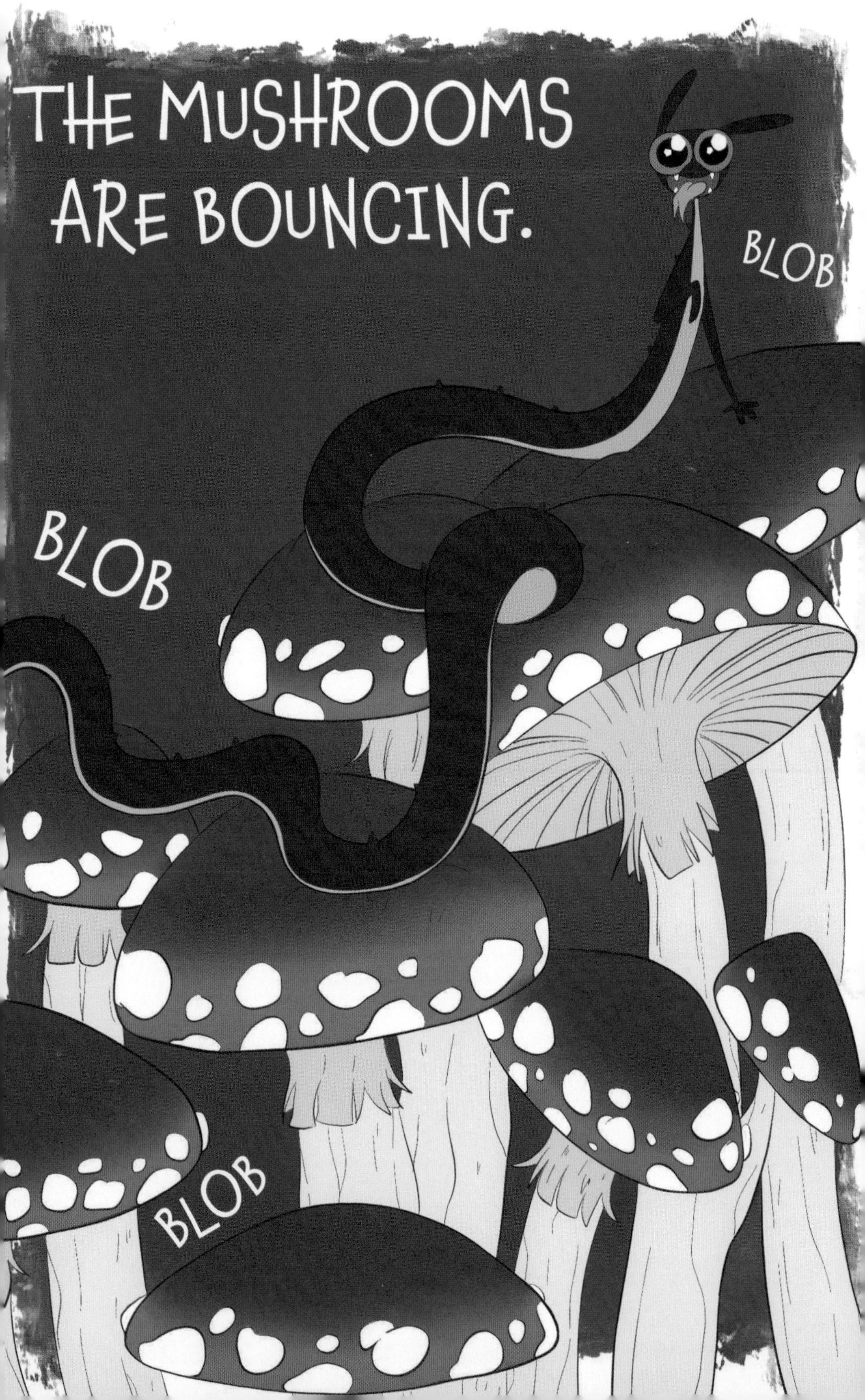
THE MUSHROOMS ARE BOUNCING.
BLOB
BLOB
BLOB

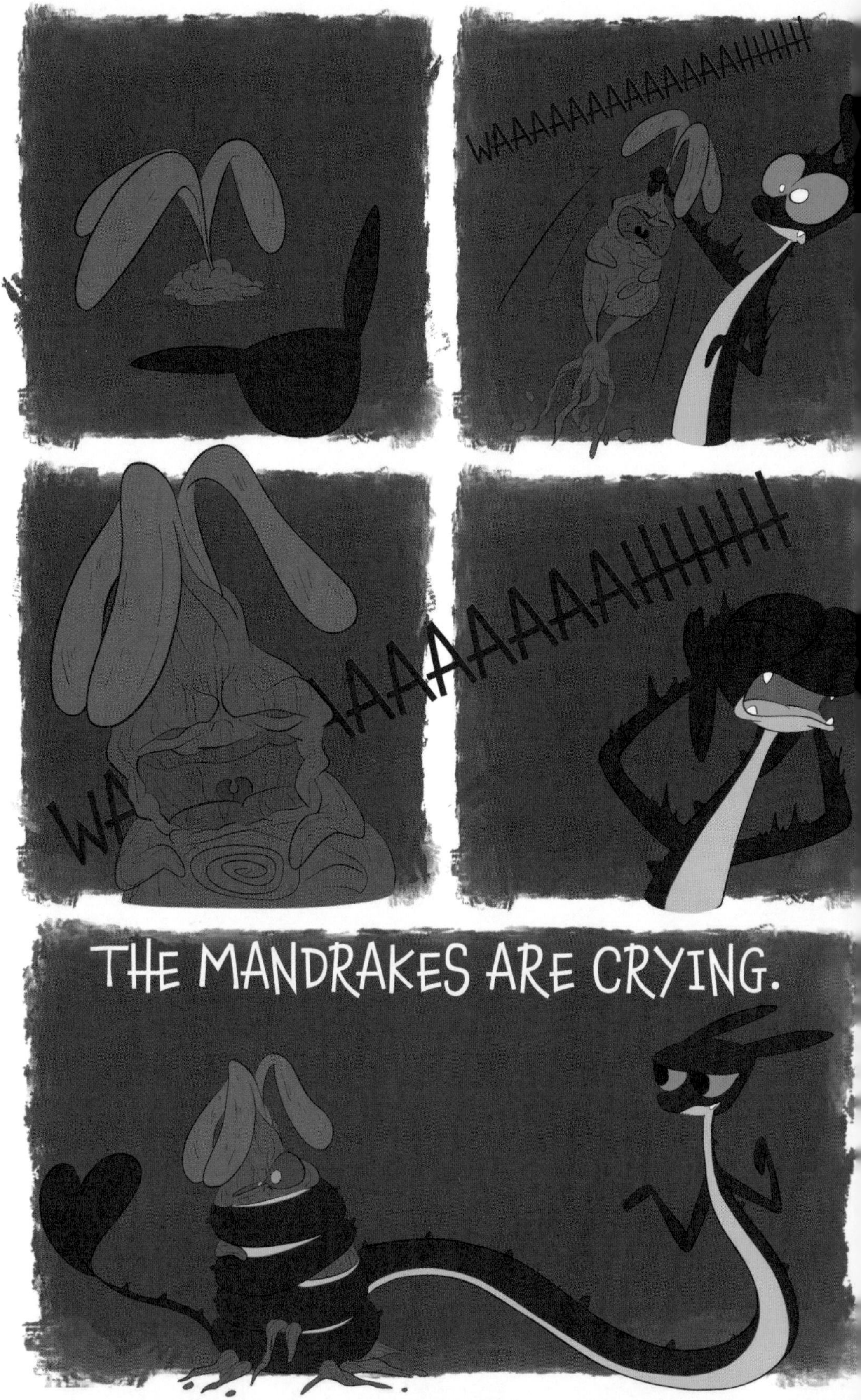
WAAAAAAAAAAAAAHHHHH
WAAAAAAAAAAAHHHHHH
THE MANDRAKES ARE CRYING.

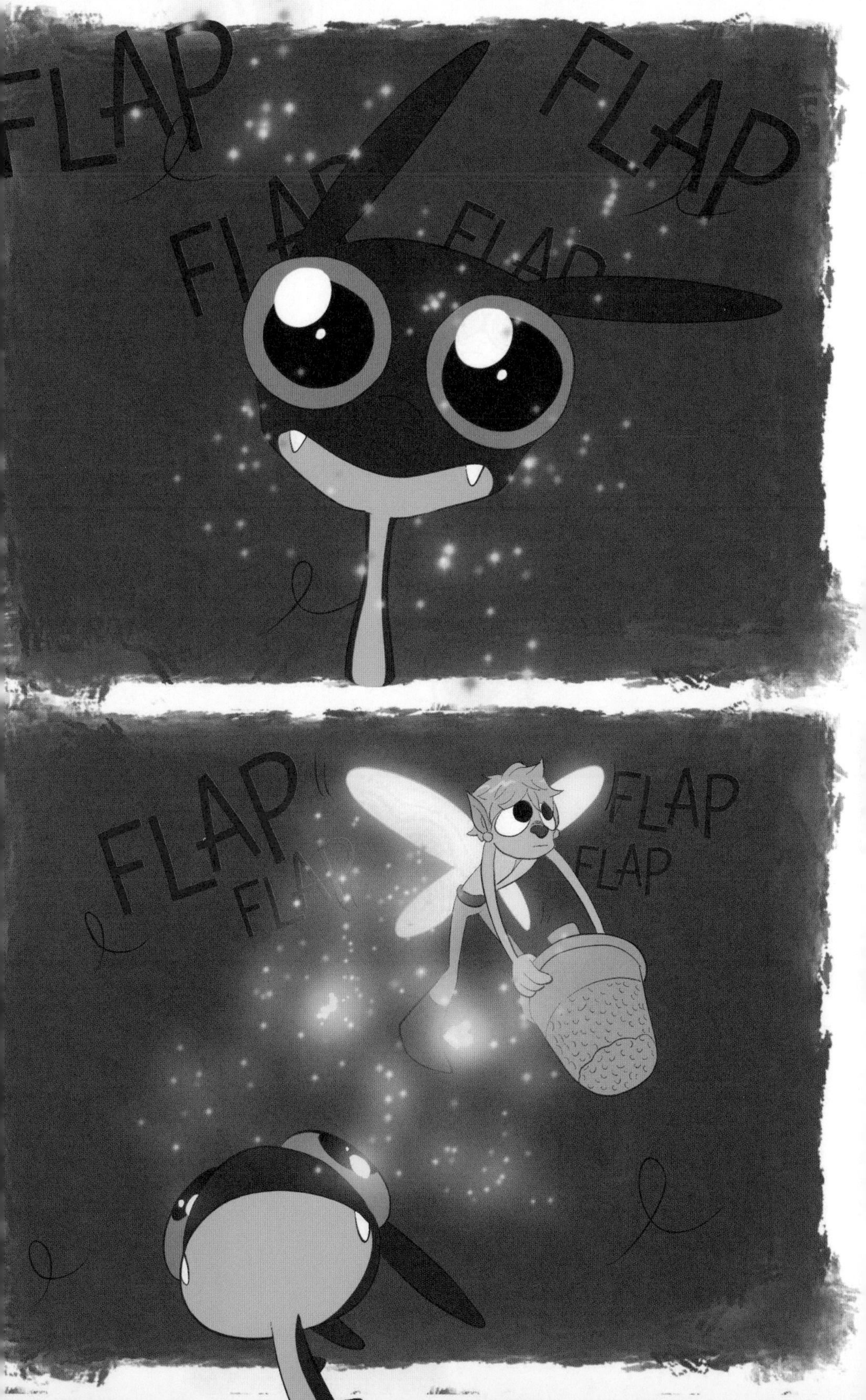
FLAP
FLAP
FLAP
FLAP
FLAP

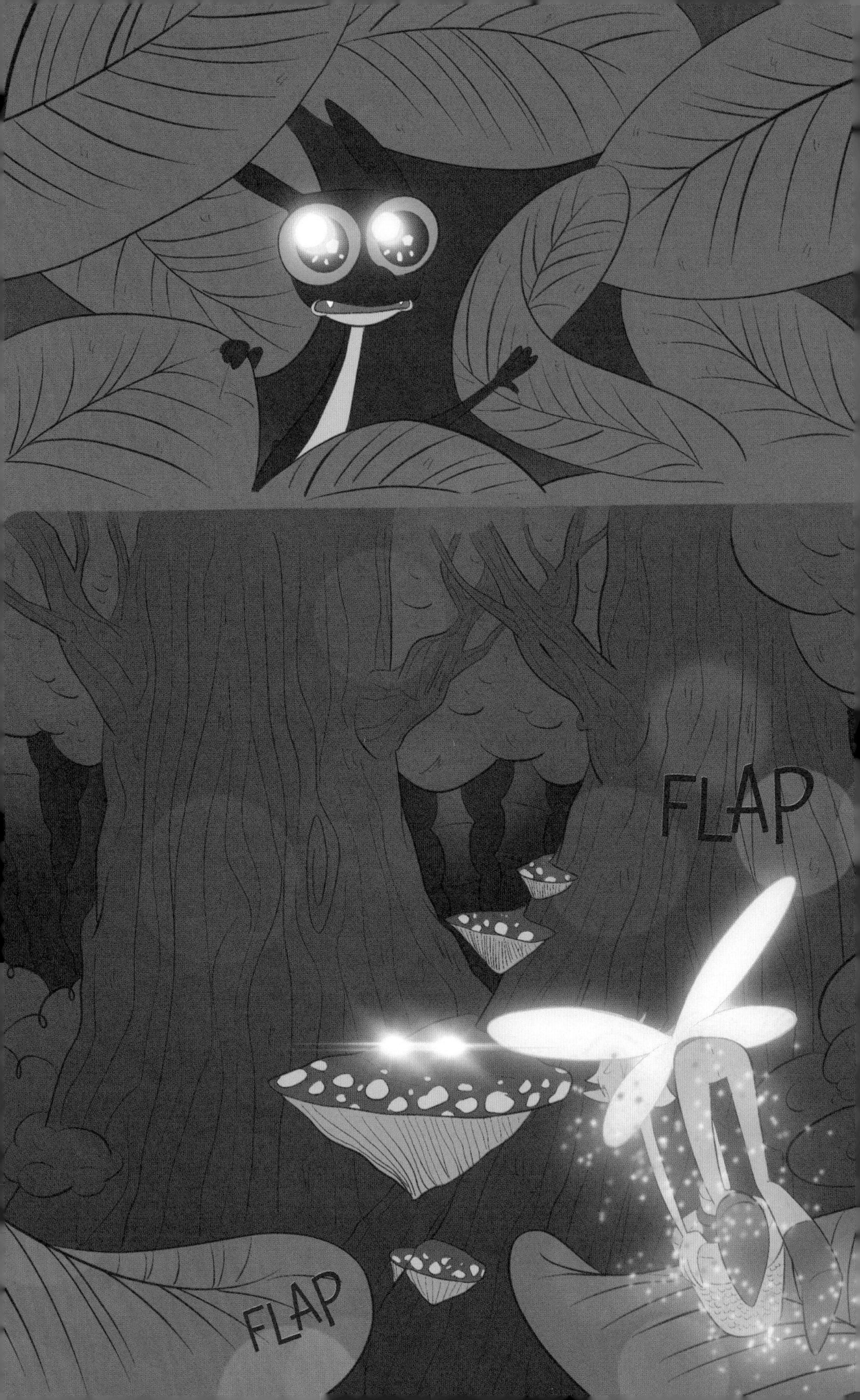
FLAP
FLAP

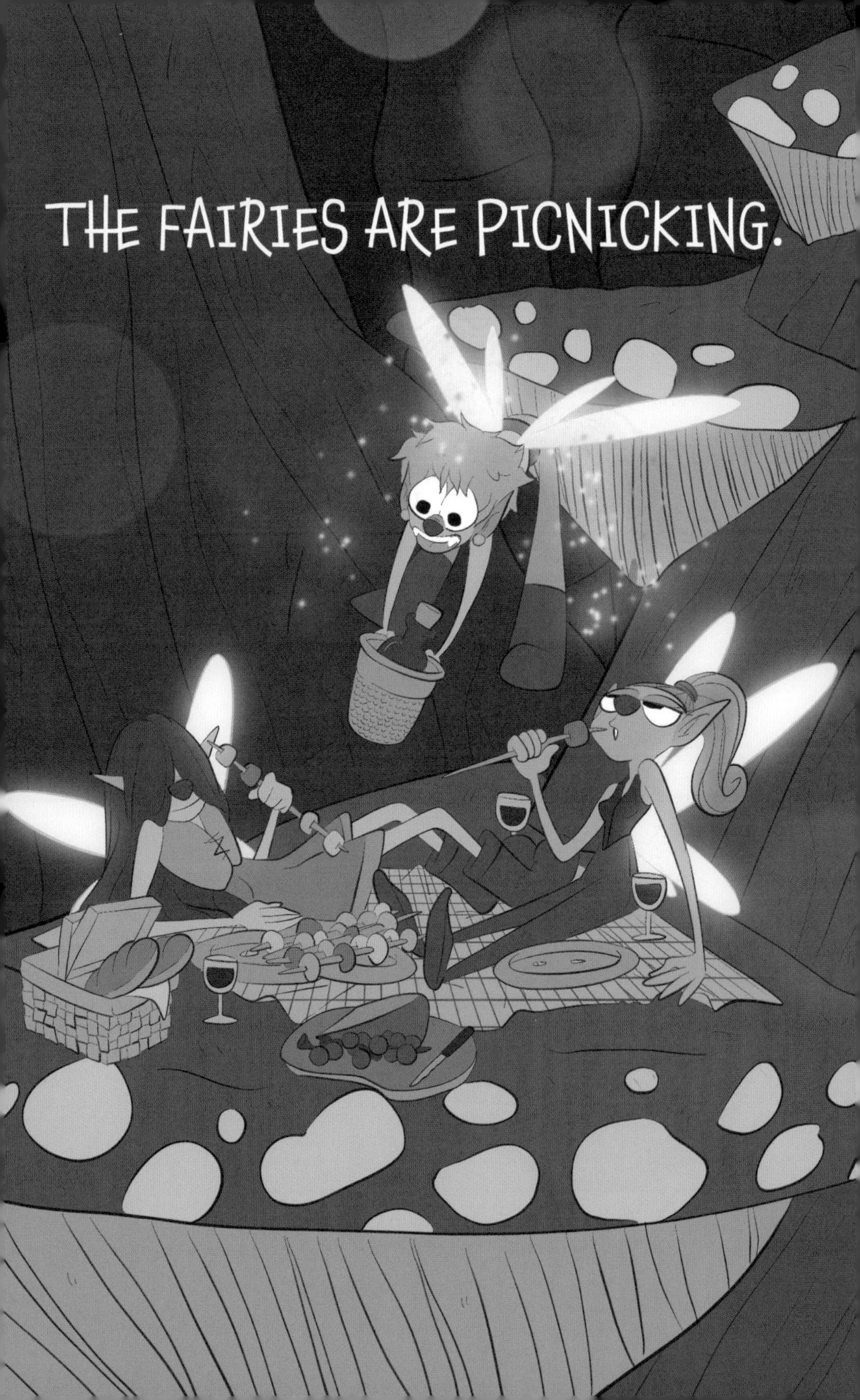
THE FAIRIES ARE PICNICKING.

THE FAIRIES

MEAN LOOK

BUTTERFLY
WINGS

FAIRY DUST

Their fairy dust is a powerful
ingredient used in potions and
remedies, and sells for a high price,
which is why they hide in
underground villages in the forest.
Don't bother them!

THE FOREST IS TRULY MAGICAL.

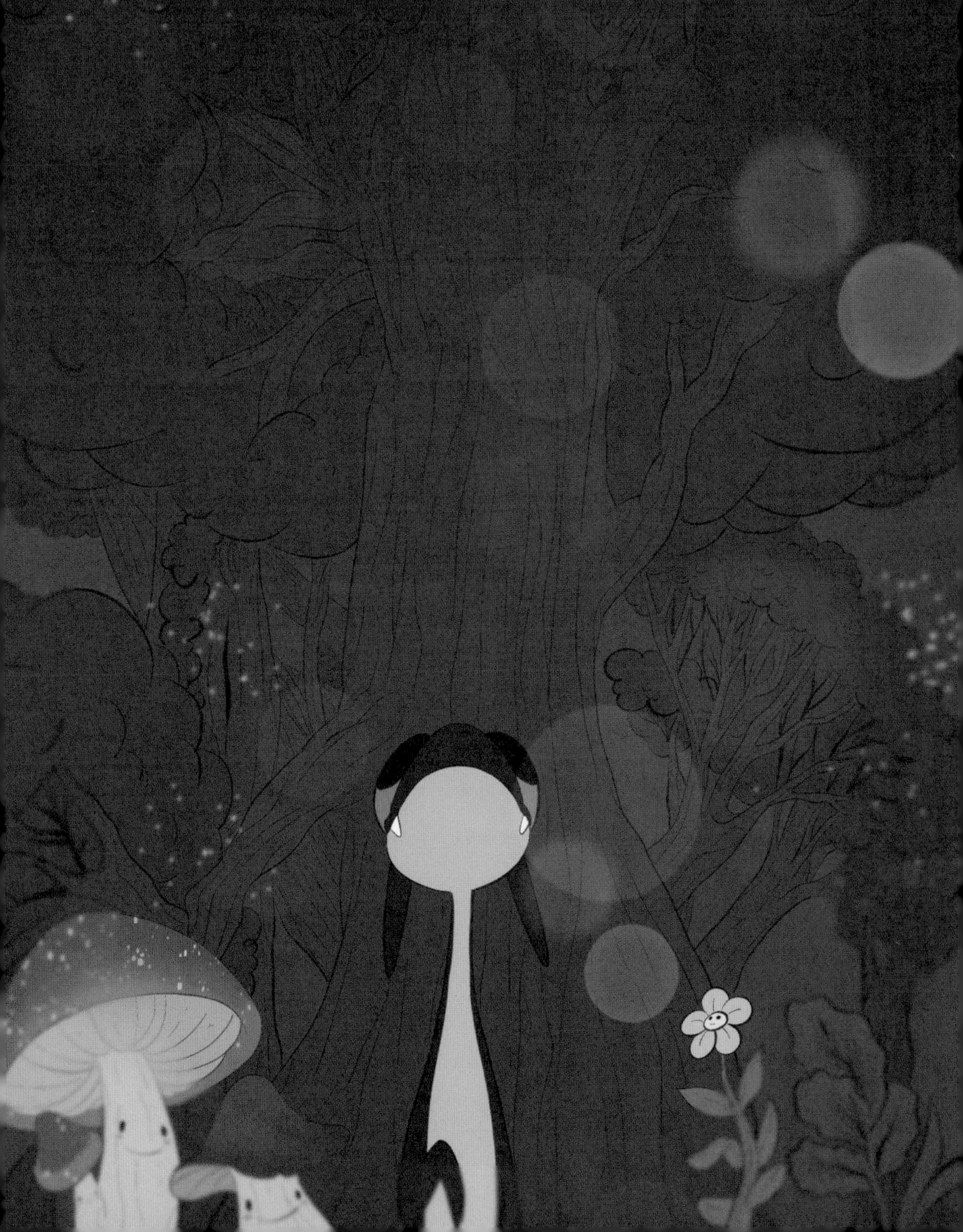

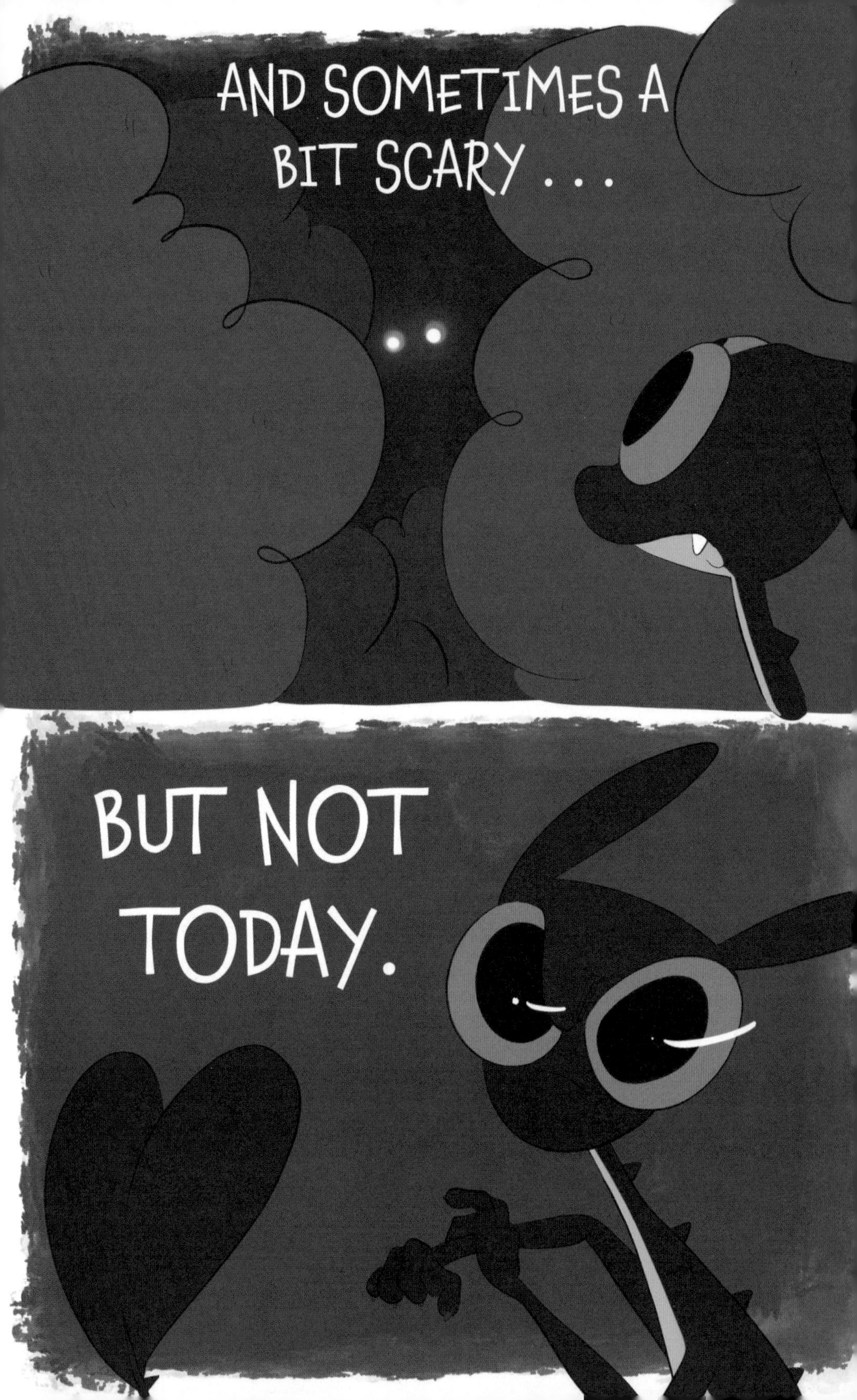
AND SOMETIMES A BIT SCARY . . .
BUT NOT TODAY.

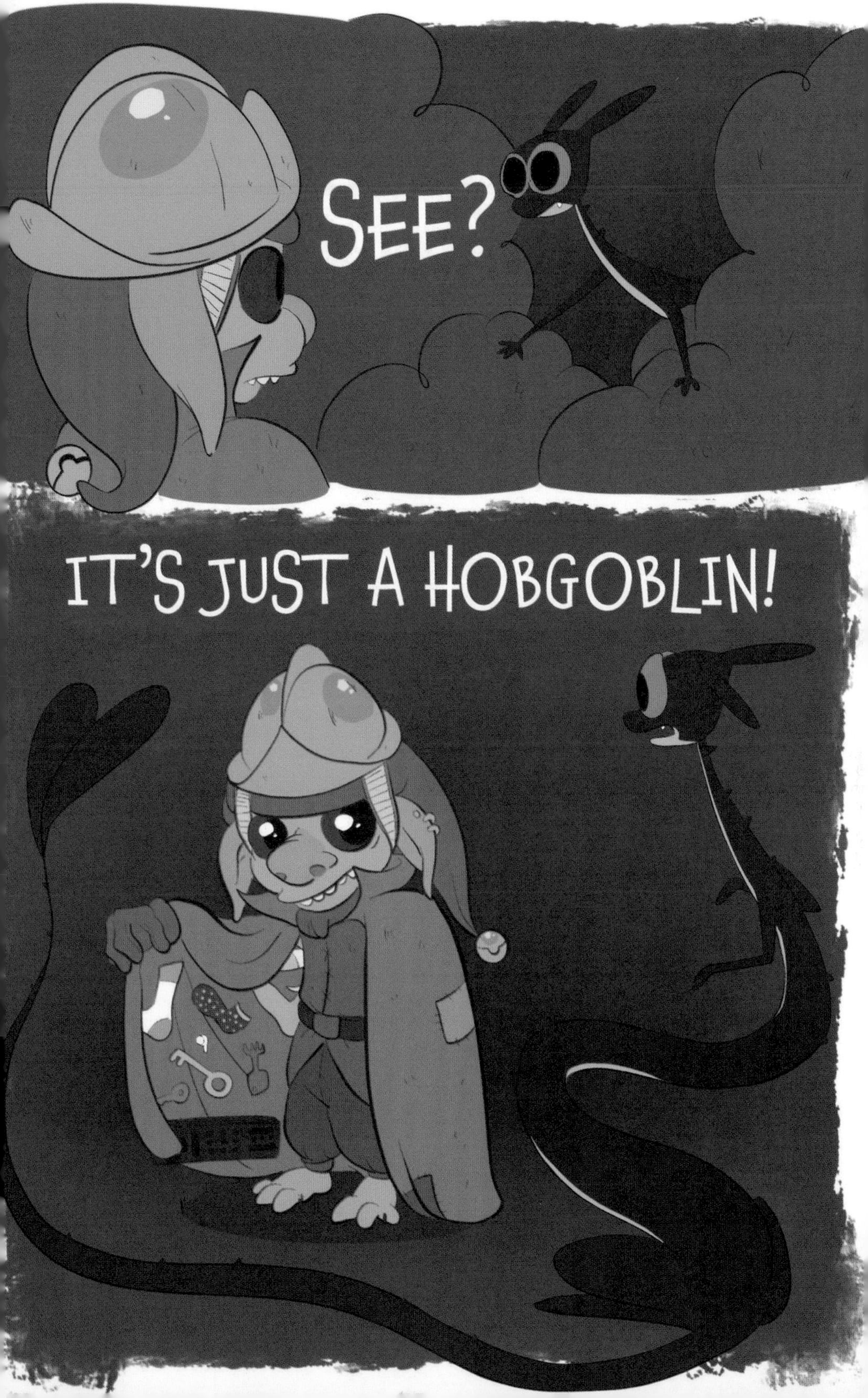
SEE?
IT'S JUST A HOBGOBLIN!

THE HOBGOBLINS

Are small things going missing in your house? Chances are a hobgoblin is in the neighborhood! These little gnomes love to steal and collect mundane items, but only to resell them in hopes of rebuilding their homes, which were destroyed by humans.

SMALL AND LANKY BODY THAT FITS ANYWHERE

LOOKING FOR SINGLE SOCKS

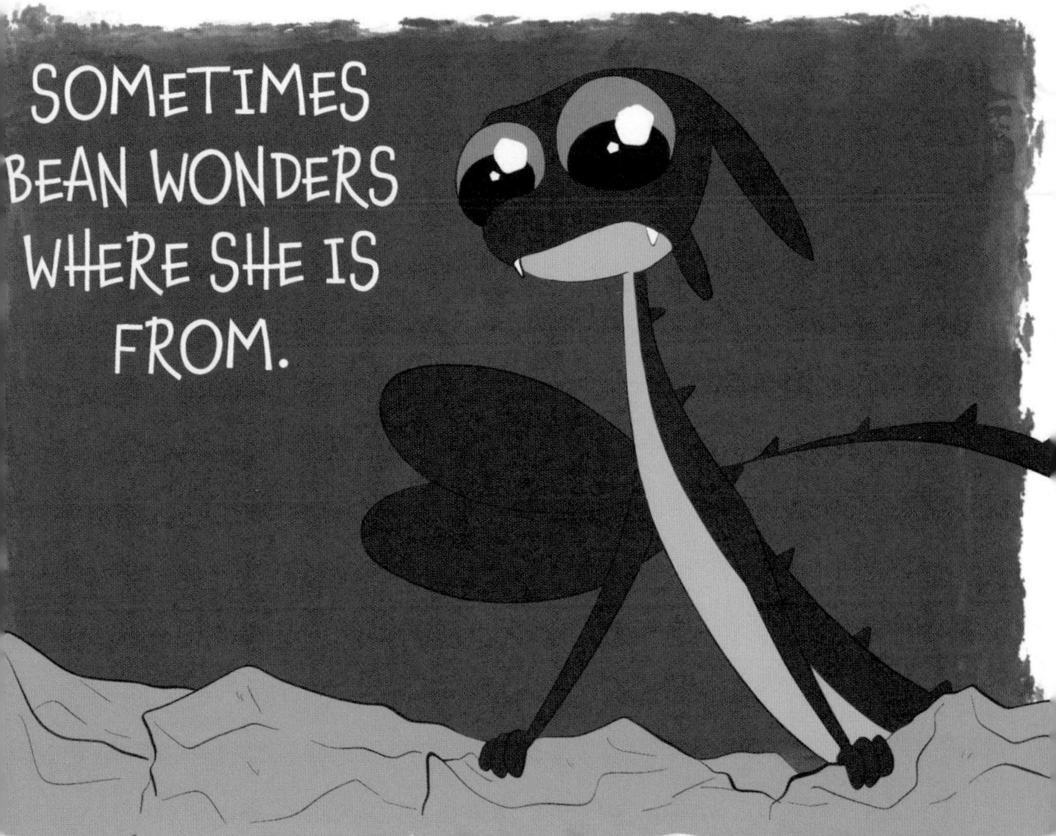
SOMETIMES BEAN WONDERS WHERE SHE IS FROM.

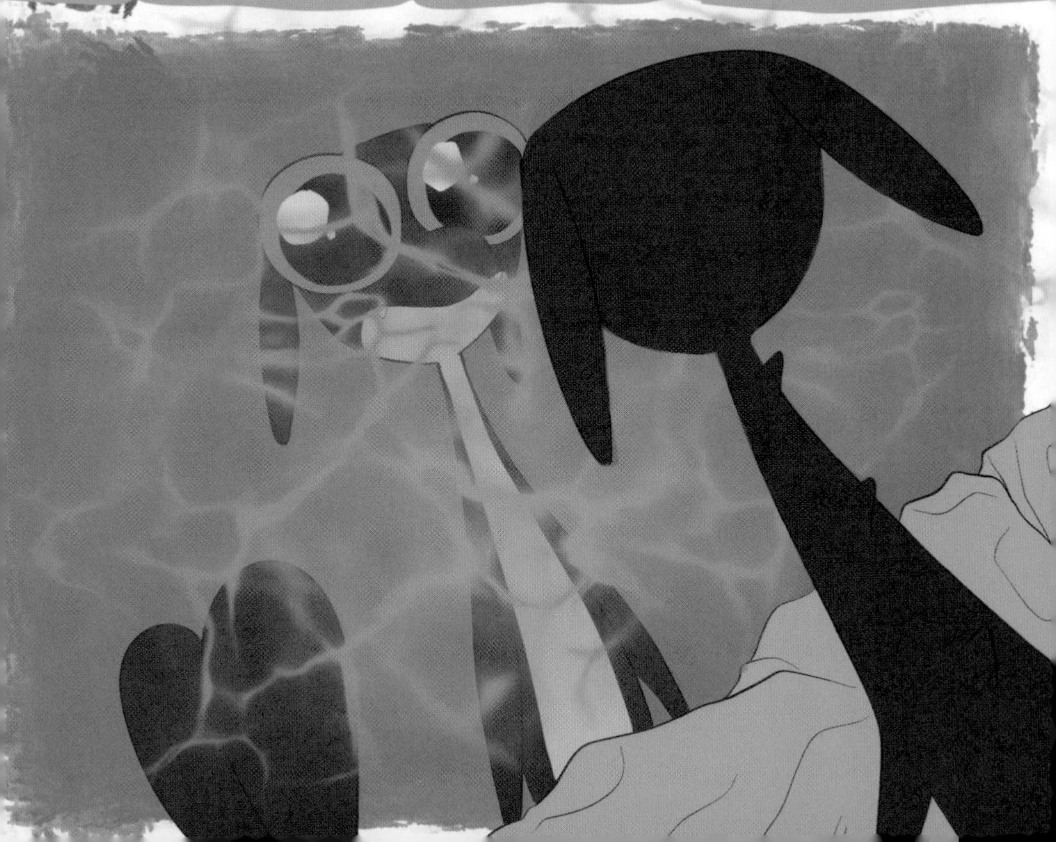

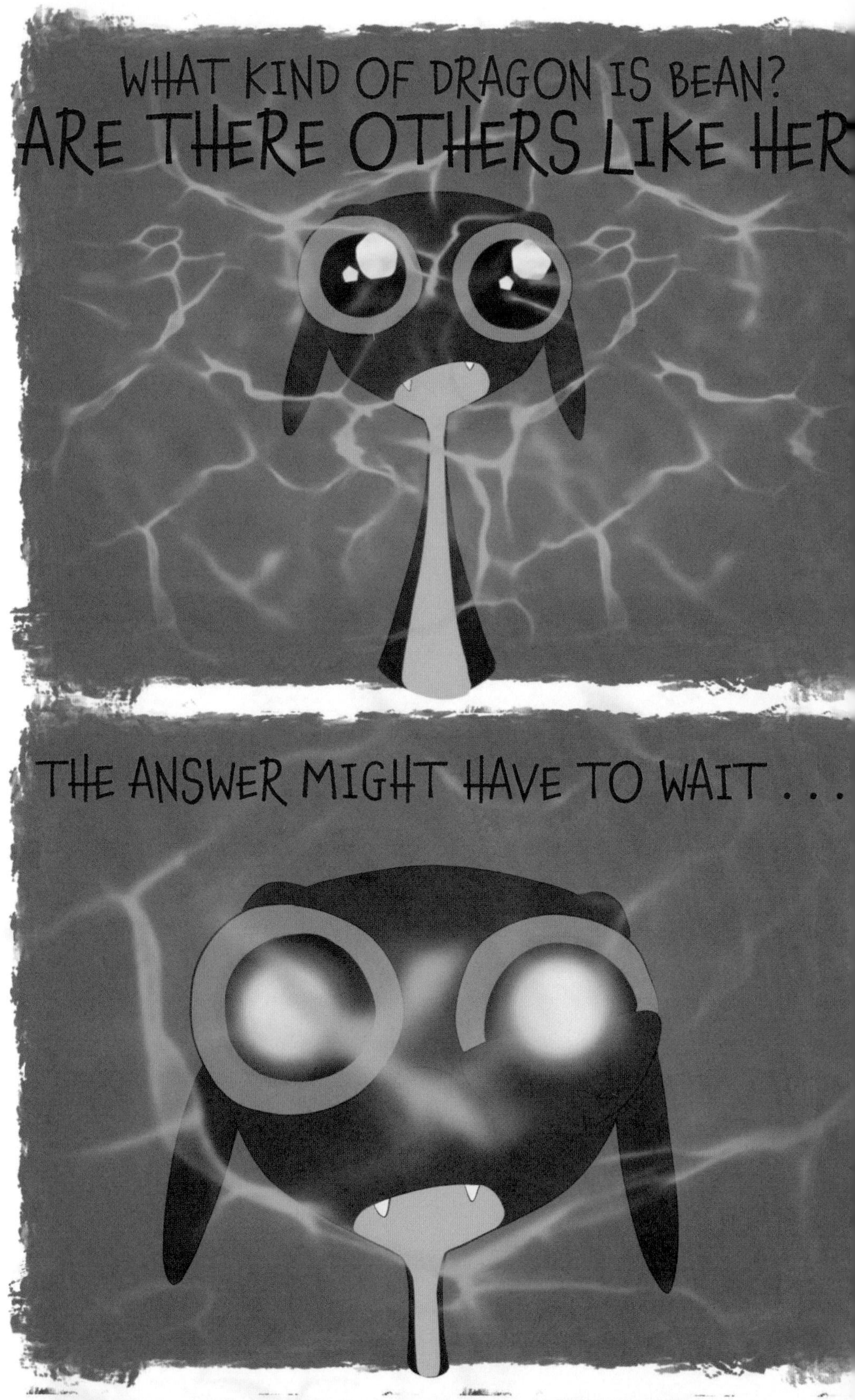
WHAT KIND OF DRAGON IS BEAN?
ARE THERE OTHERS LIKE HER
THE ANSWER MIGHT HAVE TO WAIT . . .

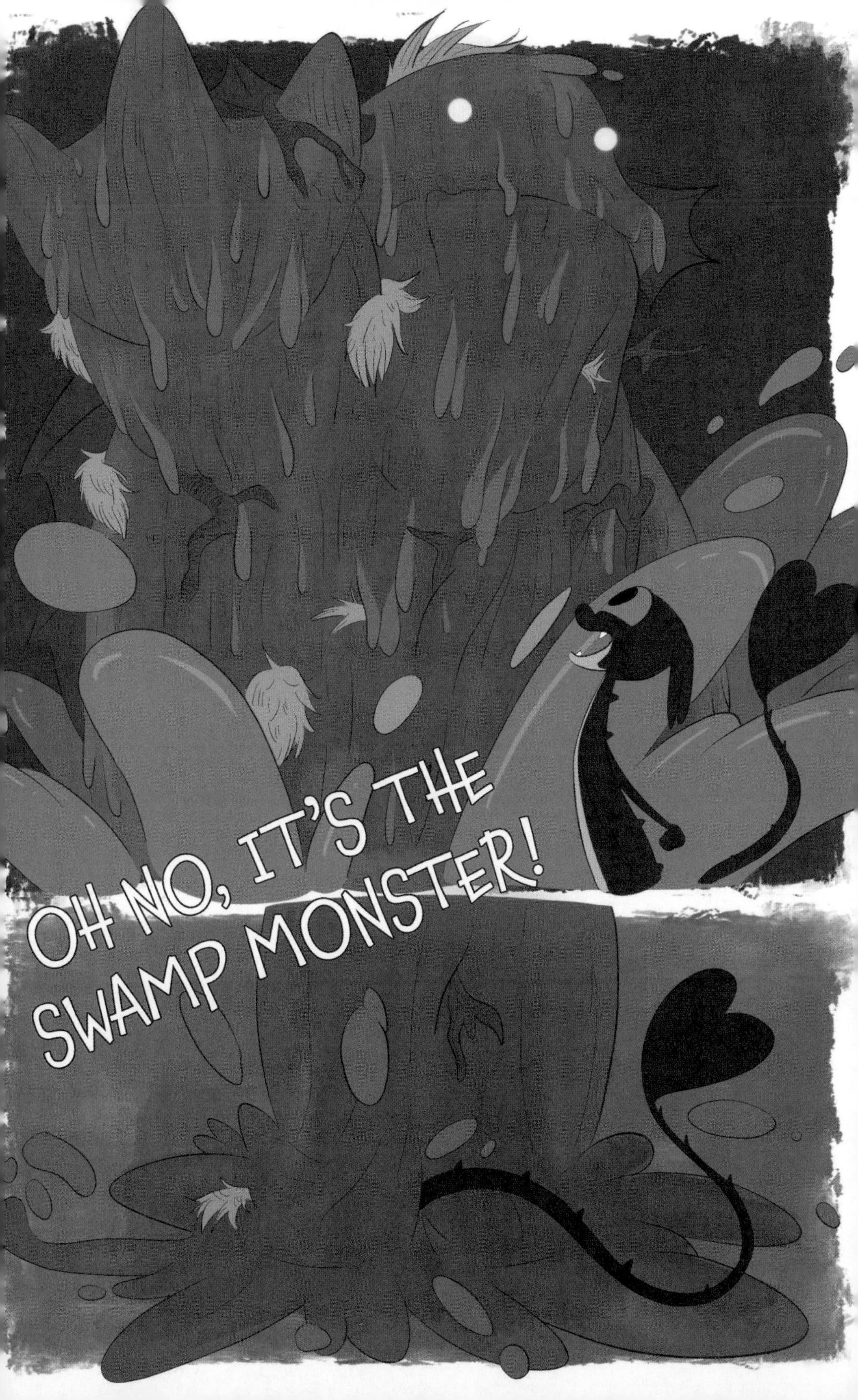
OH NO, IT'S THE SWAMP MONSTER!

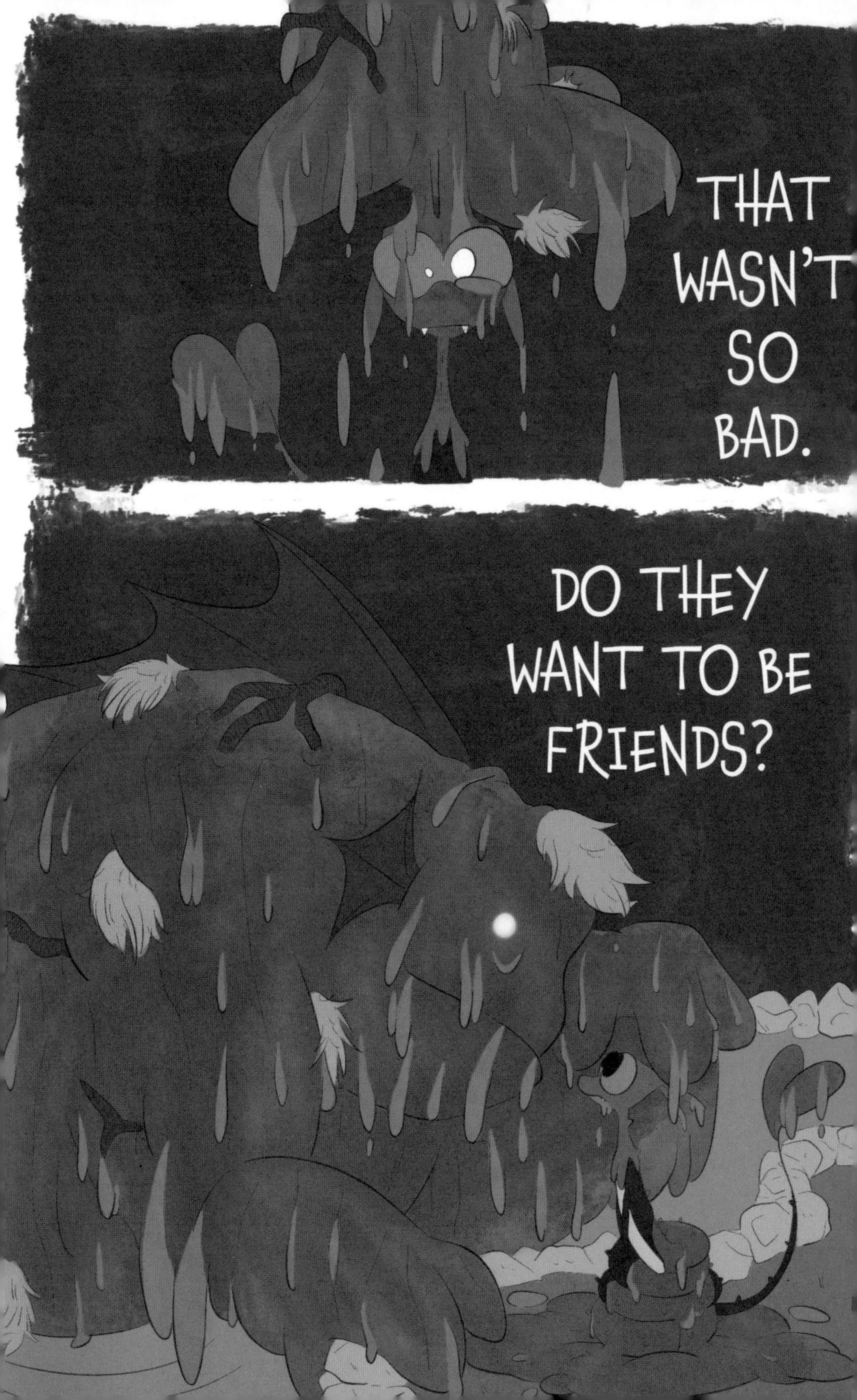
THAT WASN'T SO BAD.
DO THEY WANT TO BE FRIENDS?

THE SWAMP MONSTER

MOSS

GILLS

GLOWING EYES

PALMED FEET

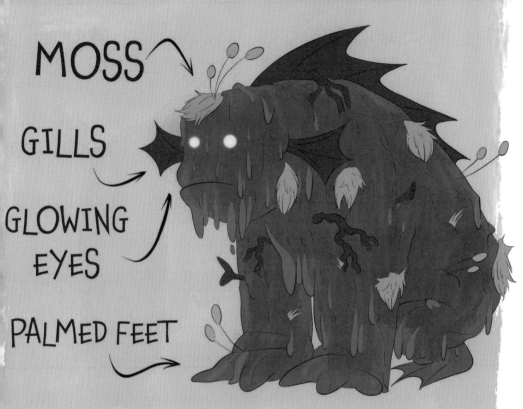

A gentle giant that likes to live by water and plants. Once they find a good place, they adapt to become part of the fauna and flora. But climate change is making it harder and harder to find a spot.

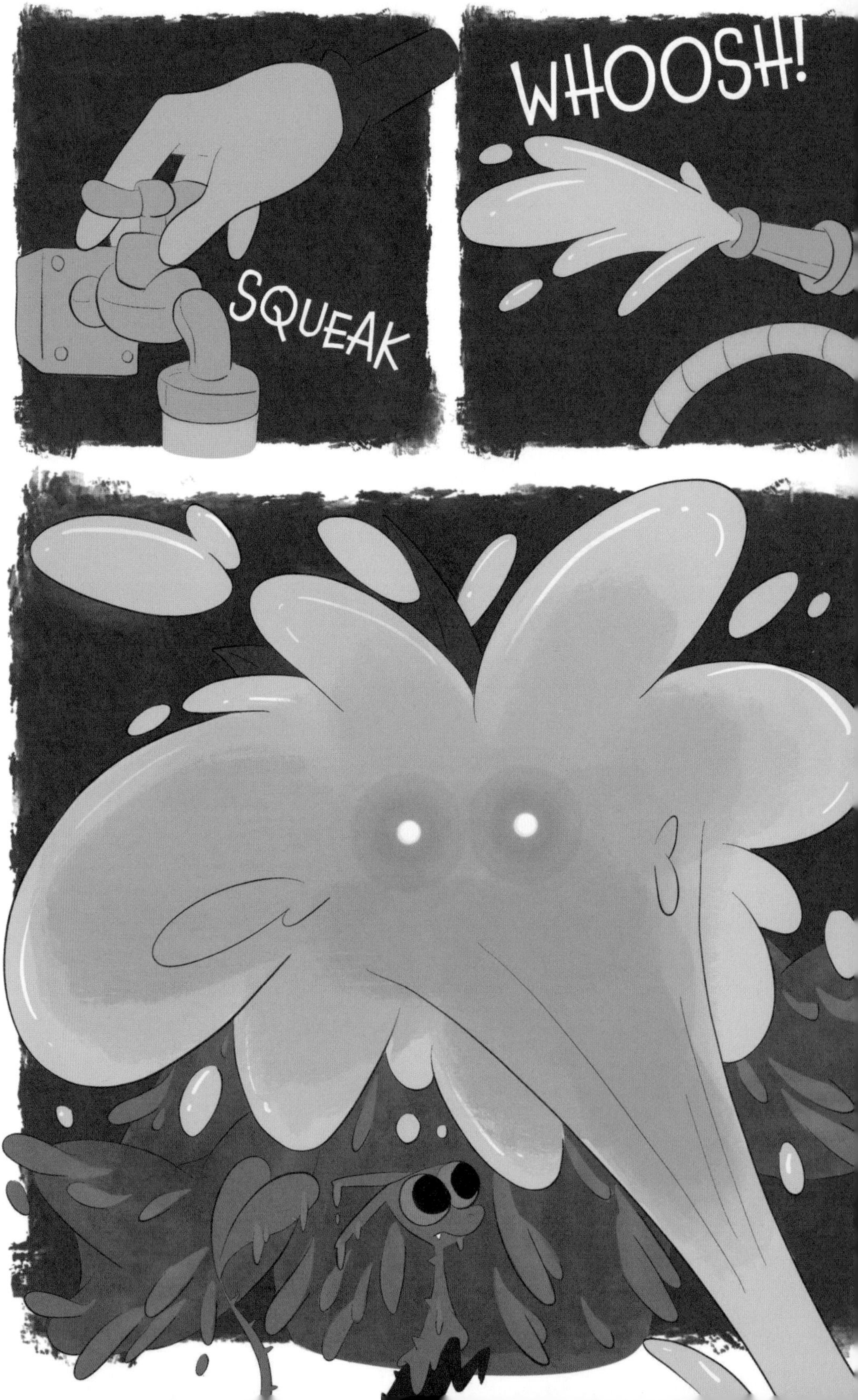
SQUEAK
WHOOSH!

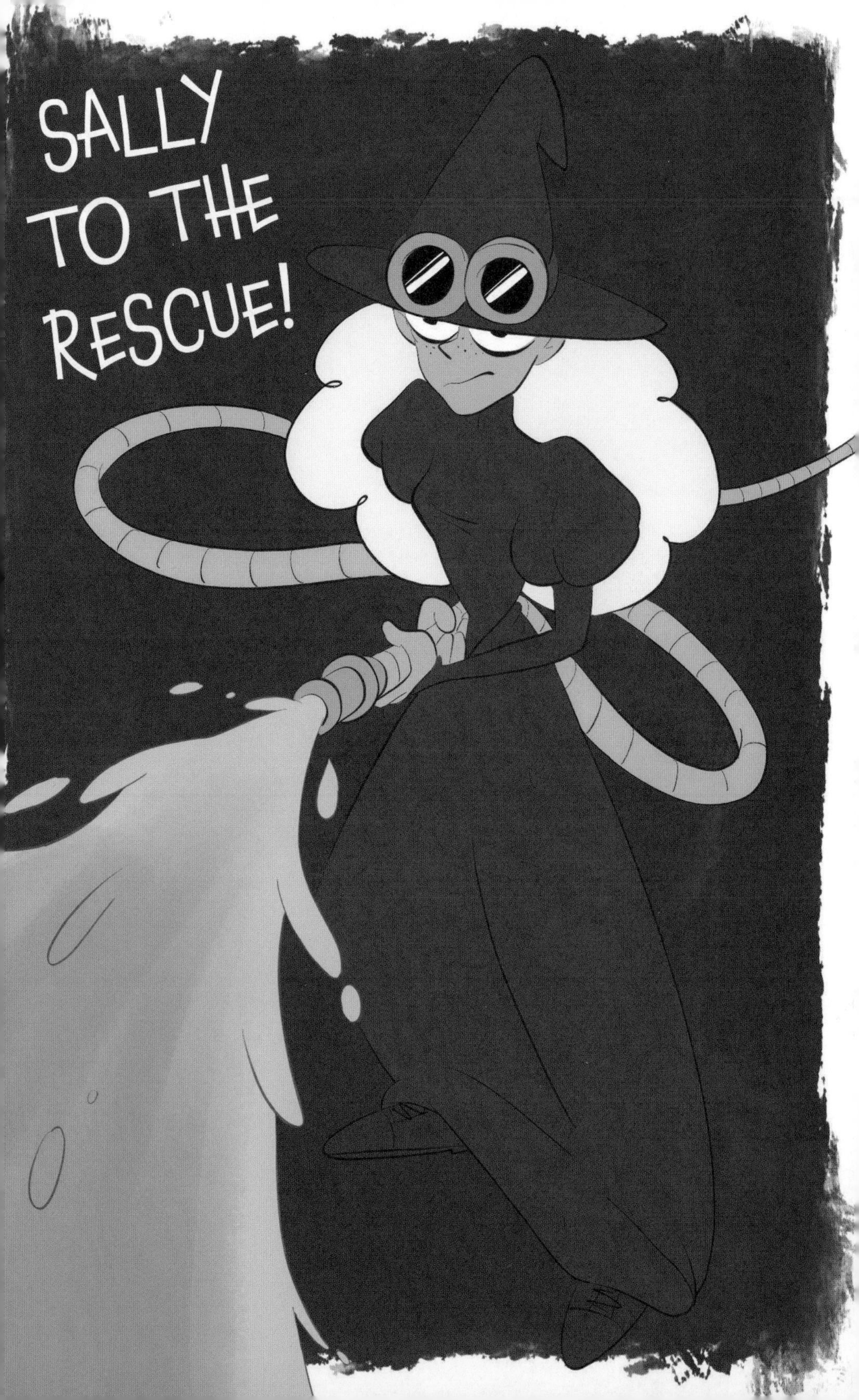
SALLY TO THE RESCUE!

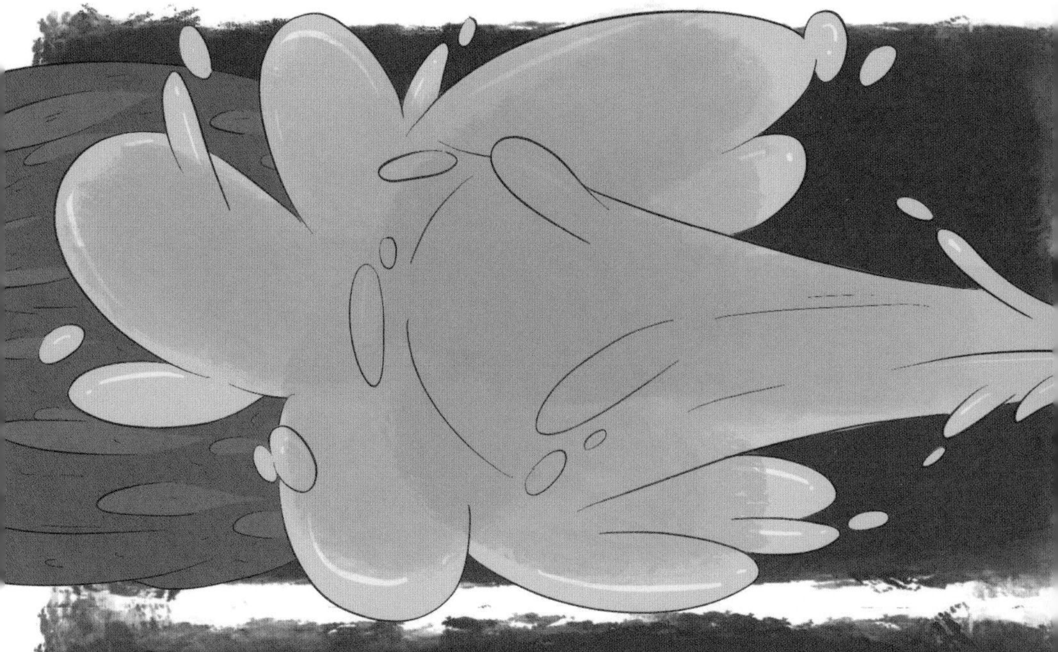
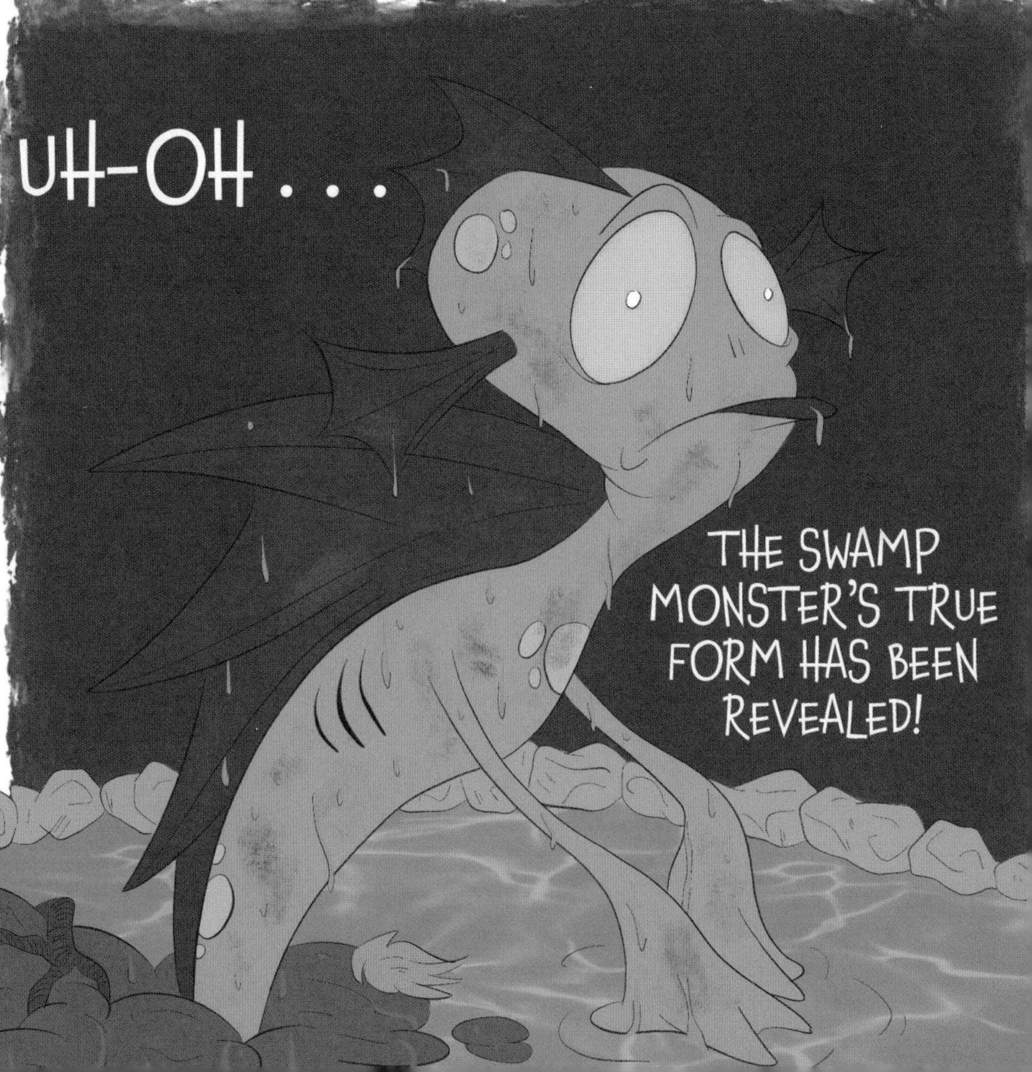
UH-OH . . .
THE SWAMP MONSTER'S TRUE FORM HAS BEEN REVEALED!

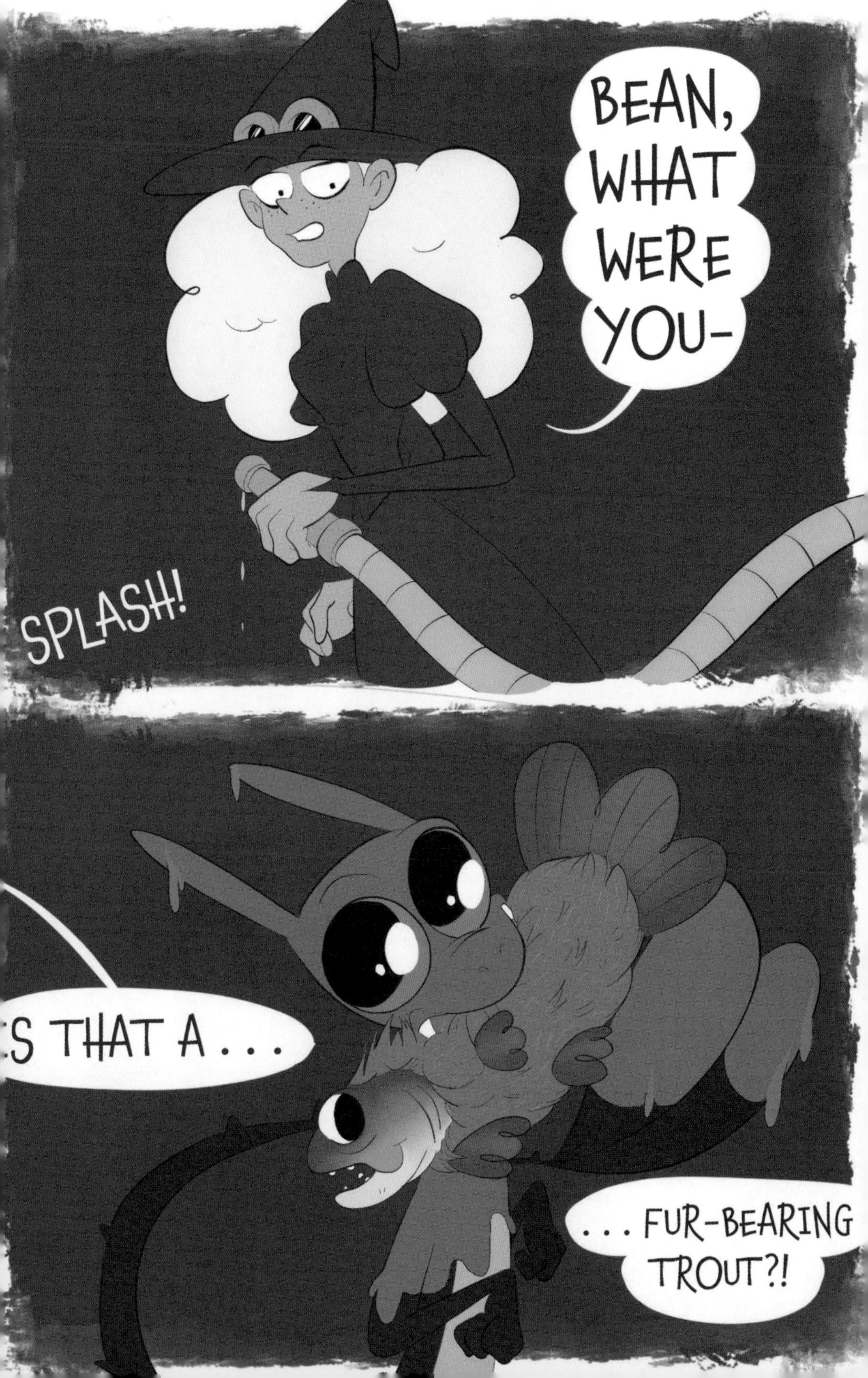
BEAN, WHAT WERE YOU-
SPLASH!
S THAT A . . .
. . . FUR-BEARING TROUT?!

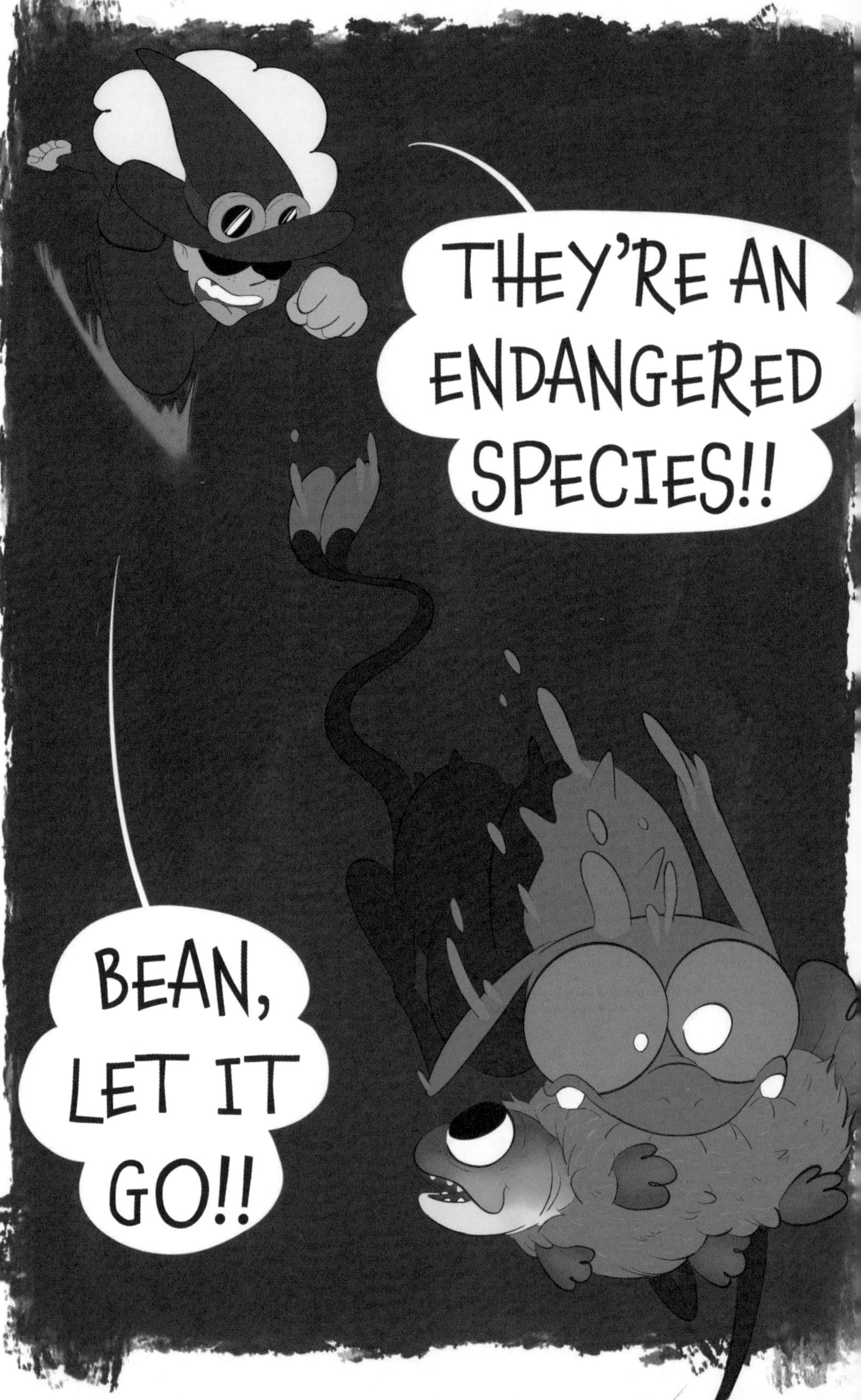
THEY'RE AN ENDANGERED SPECIES!!
BEAN, LET IT GO!!

THE FUR-BEARING TROUT

SMALL
GILLS

SOFT
FUR

WIGGLY
FIN

Just your average, regular
trout . . . but with fur.
Their fur helps them keep warm
in icy rivers all through winter
and scare off predators! But it
also makes them targets to
make luxury coats and bags.

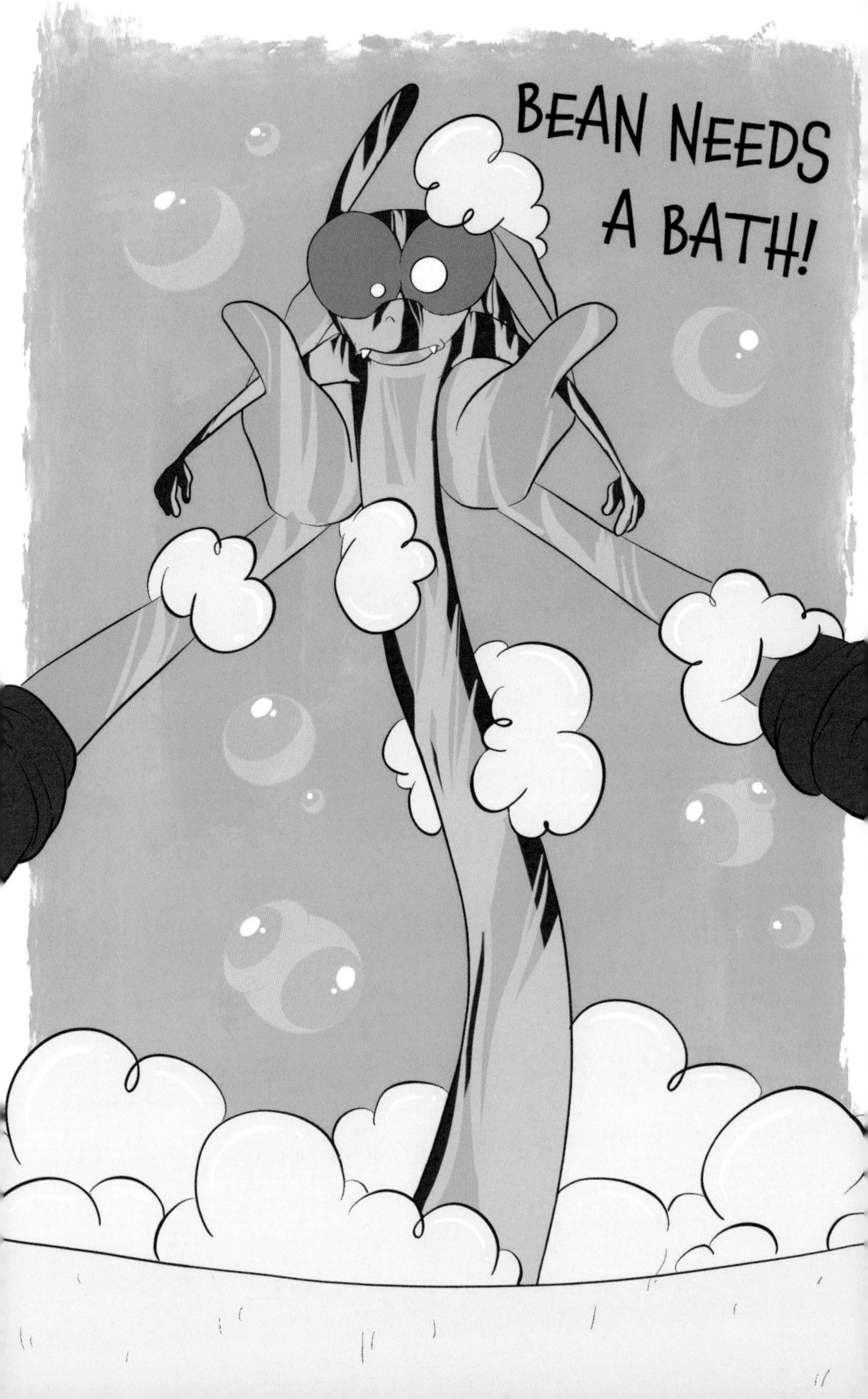
BEAN NEEDS A BATH!

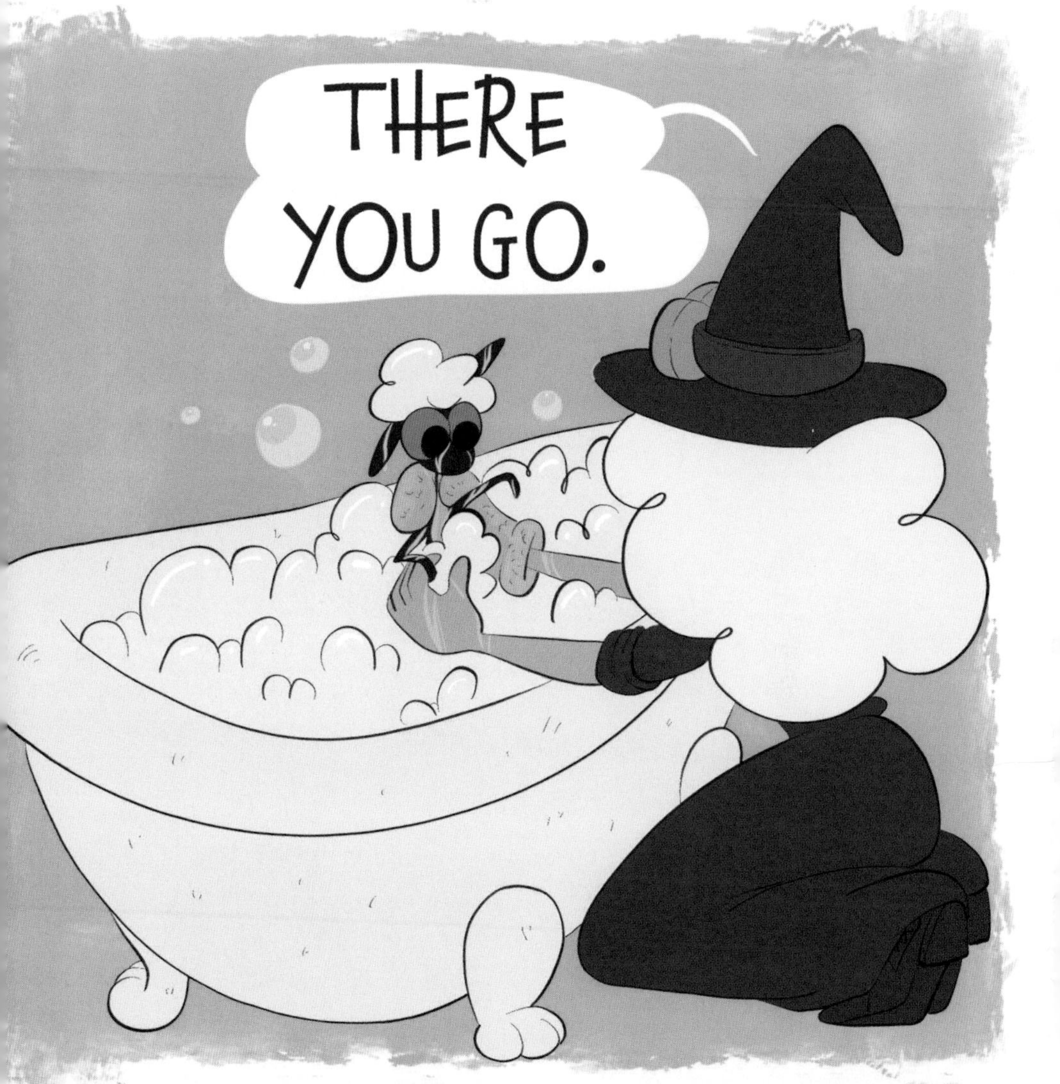
THERE YOU GO.

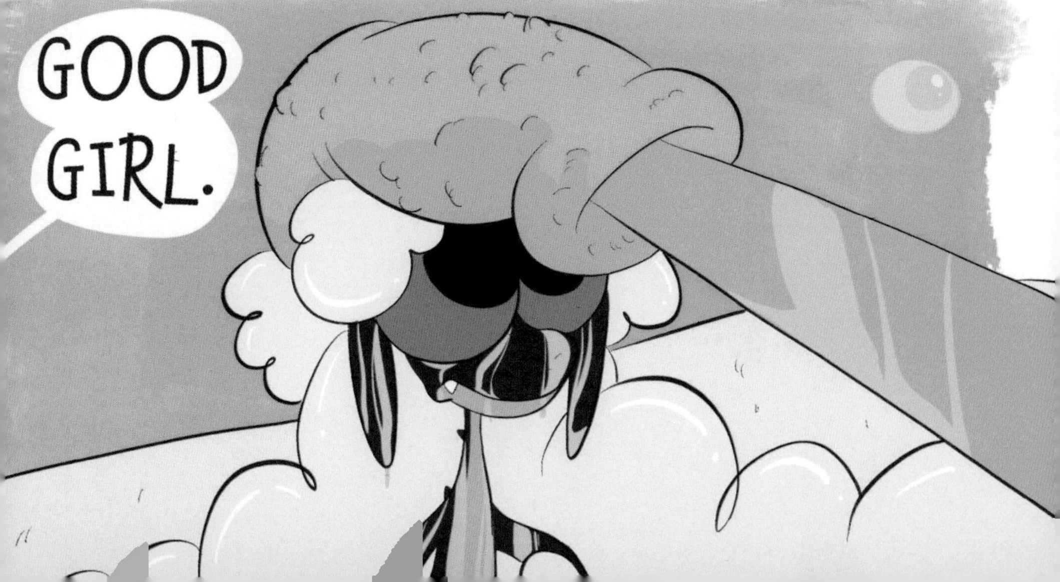
GOOD GIRL.

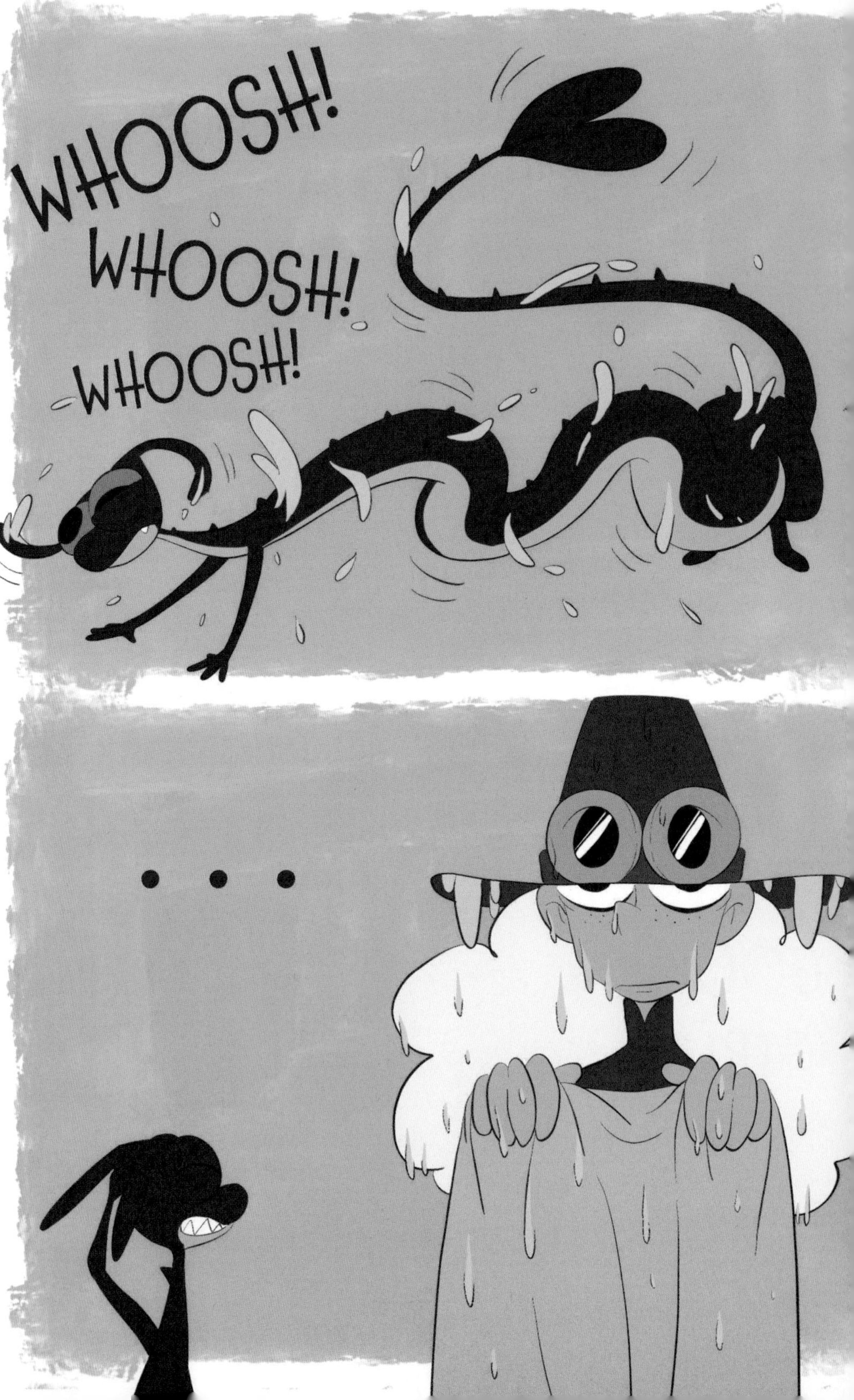
WHOOSH!
WHOOSH!
WHOOSH!
. . .

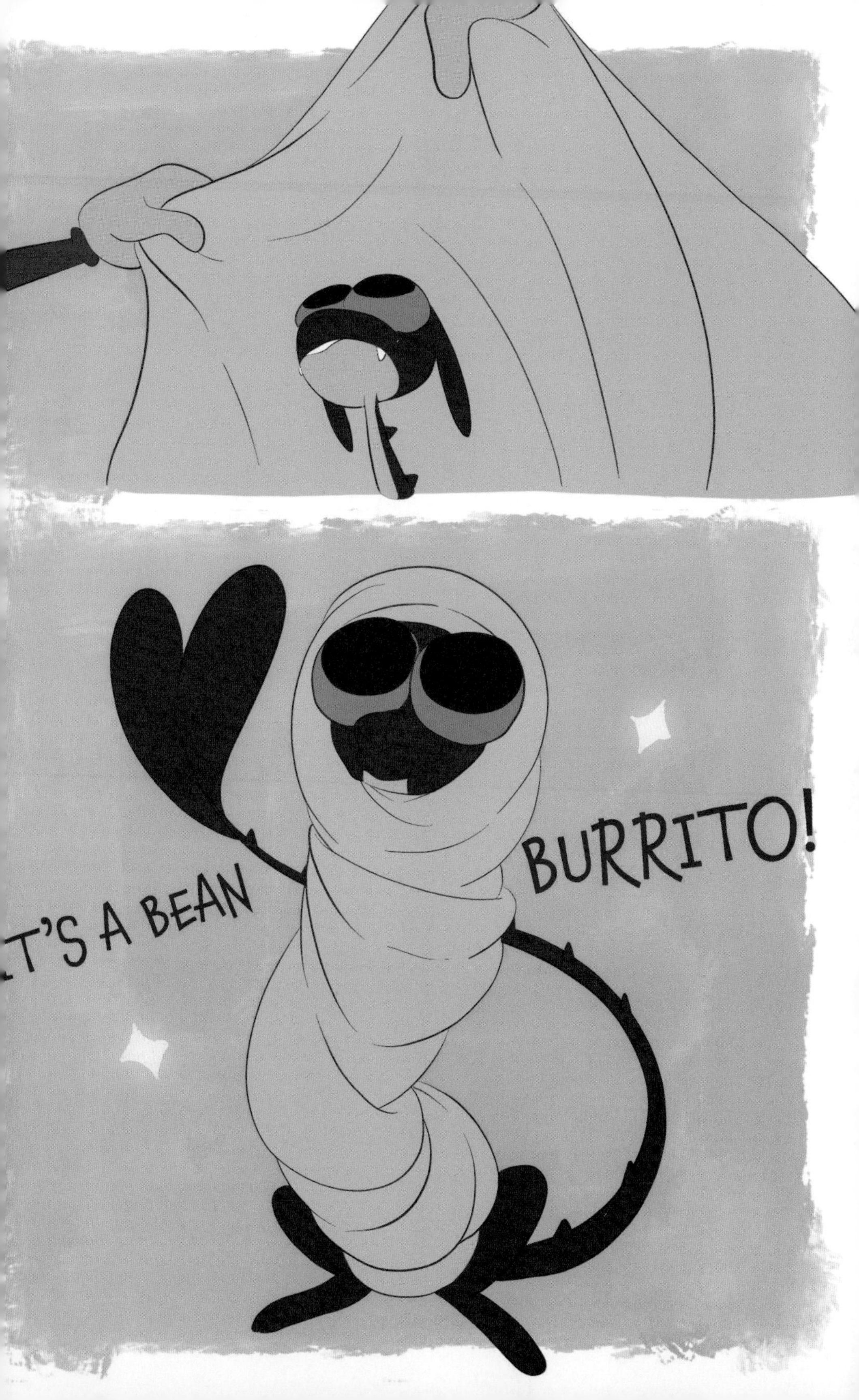
T’S A BEAN BURRITO!

SALLY

When she was little,
Sally cracked open Bean's egg
wanting to make an omelet.
They've been best friends ever since!
She is now a full-grown witch and
hardly ever leaves her
swamp.

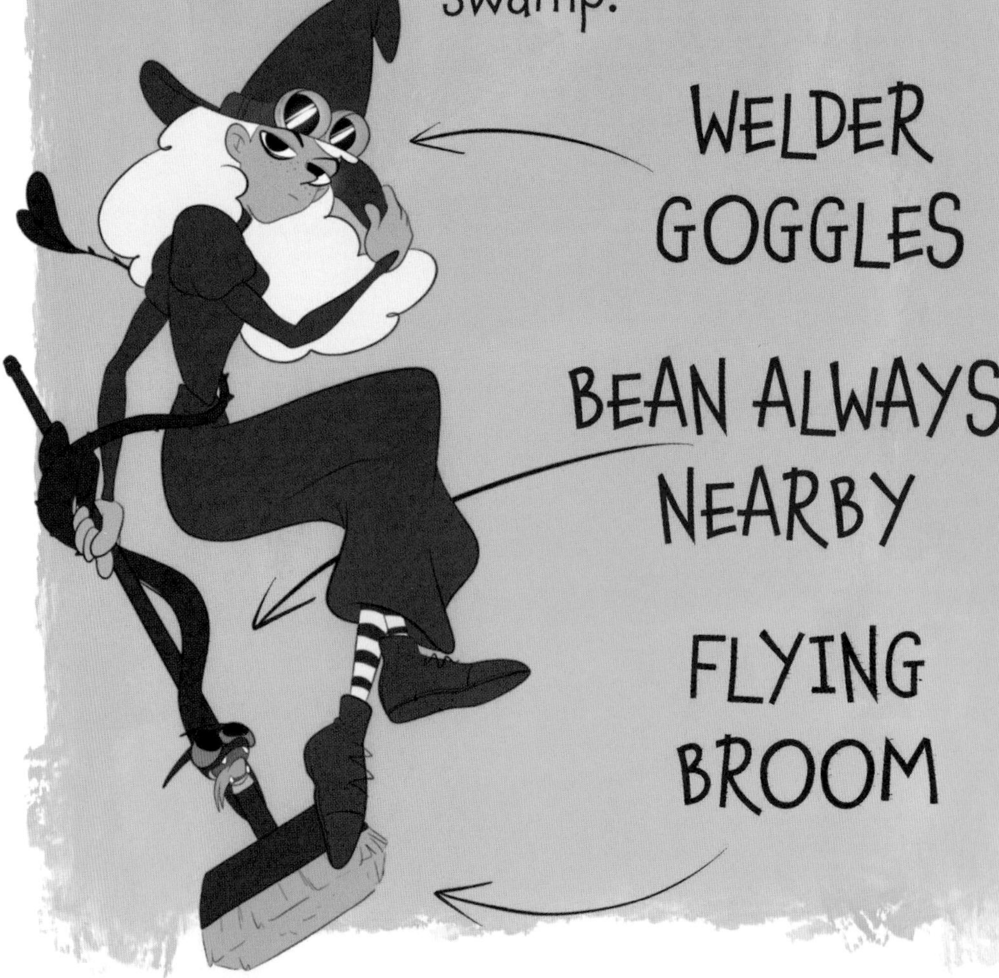
WELDER GOGGLES
BEAN ALWAYS NEARBY
FLYING BROOM

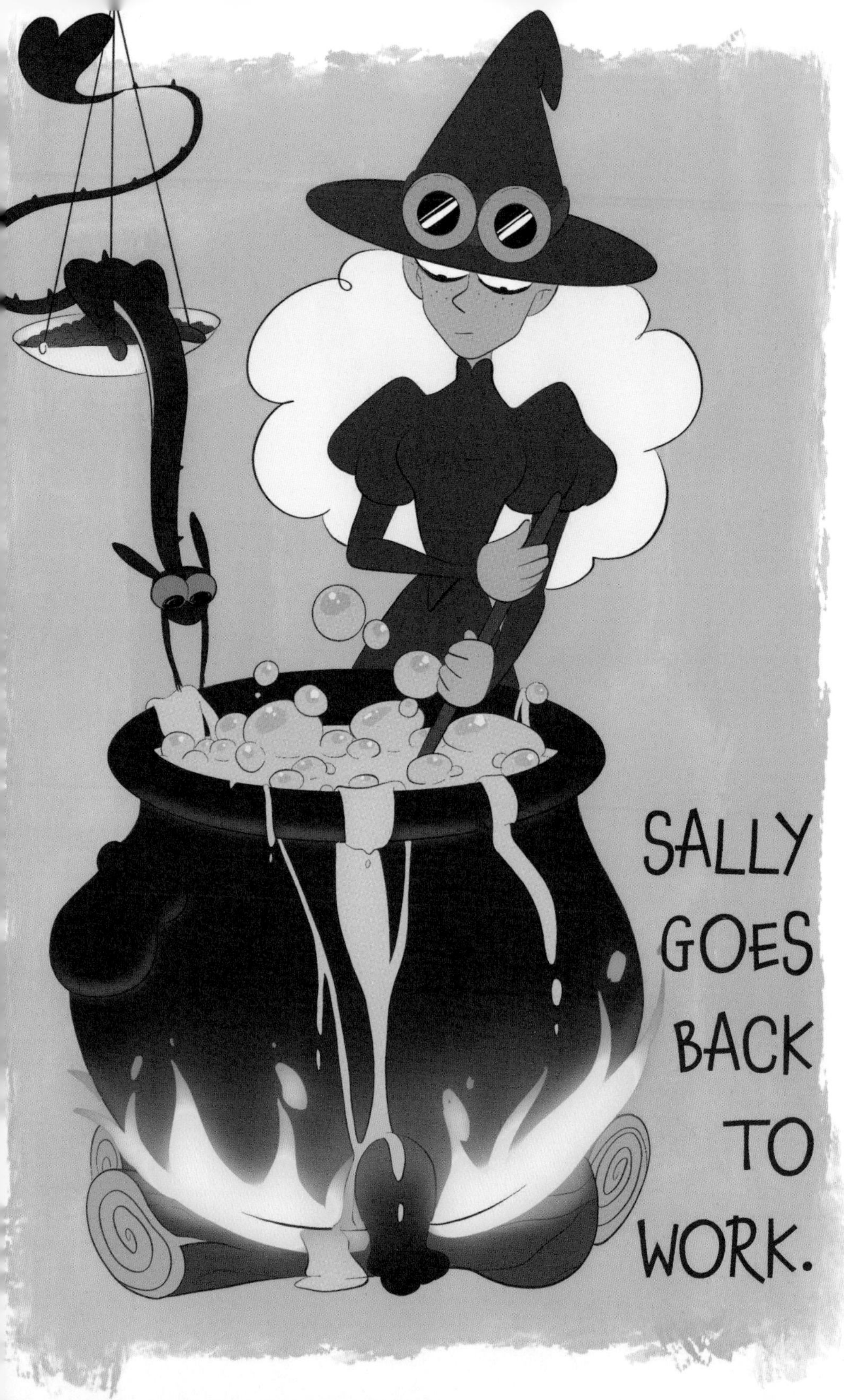
SALLY GOES BACK TO WORK.

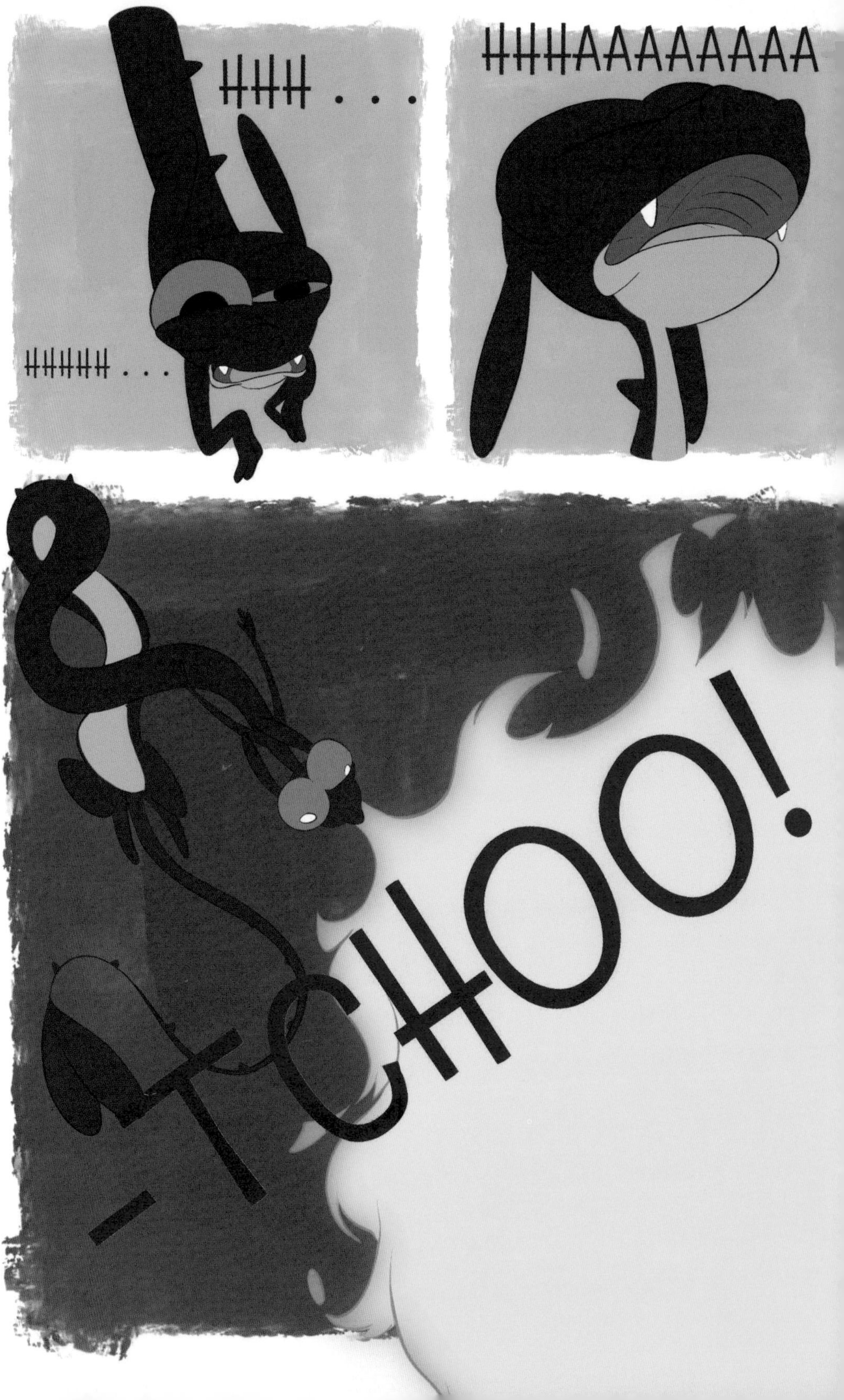
HHH . . .
HHHHH . . .
HHHAAAAAAAA
-TCHOO!

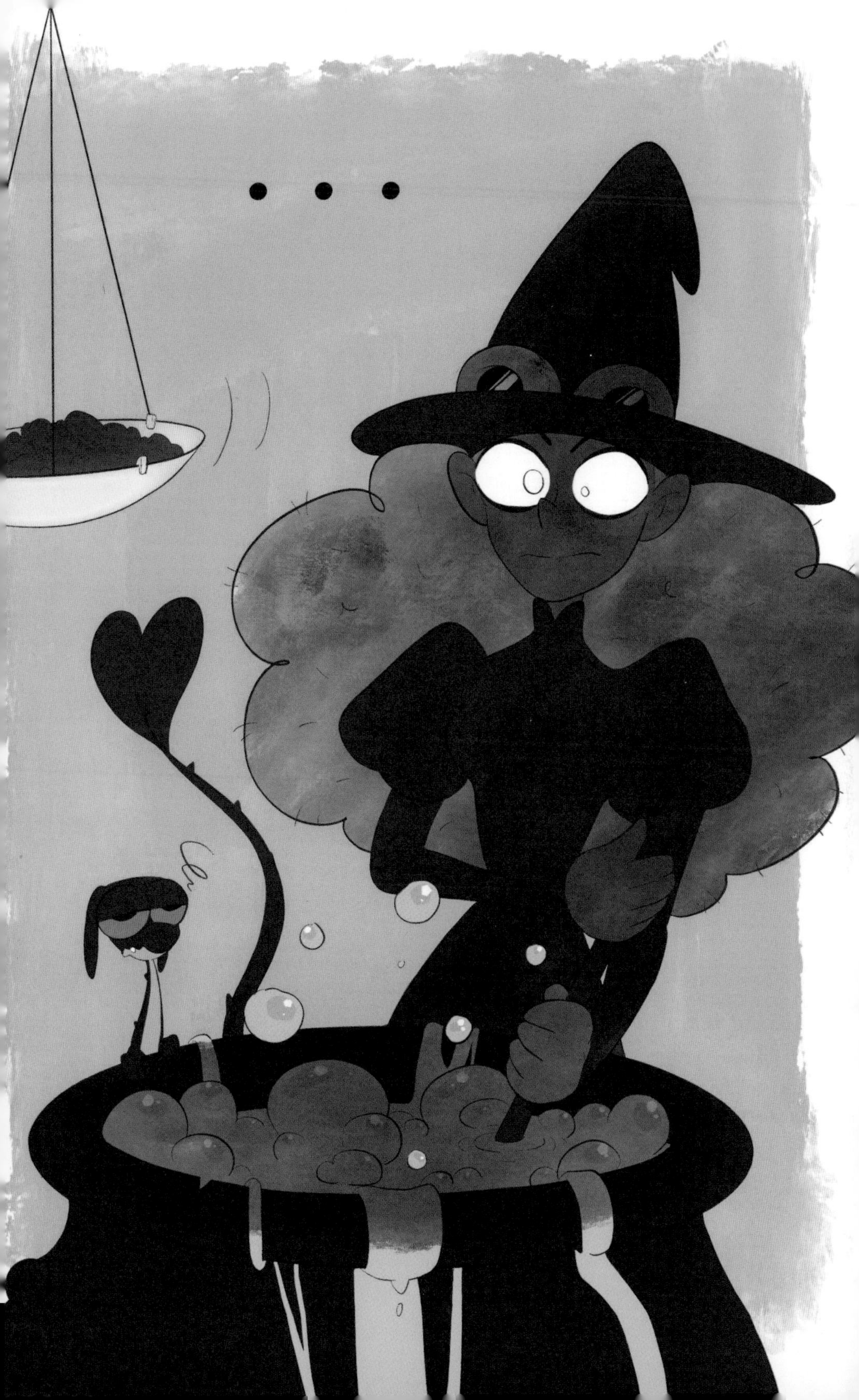

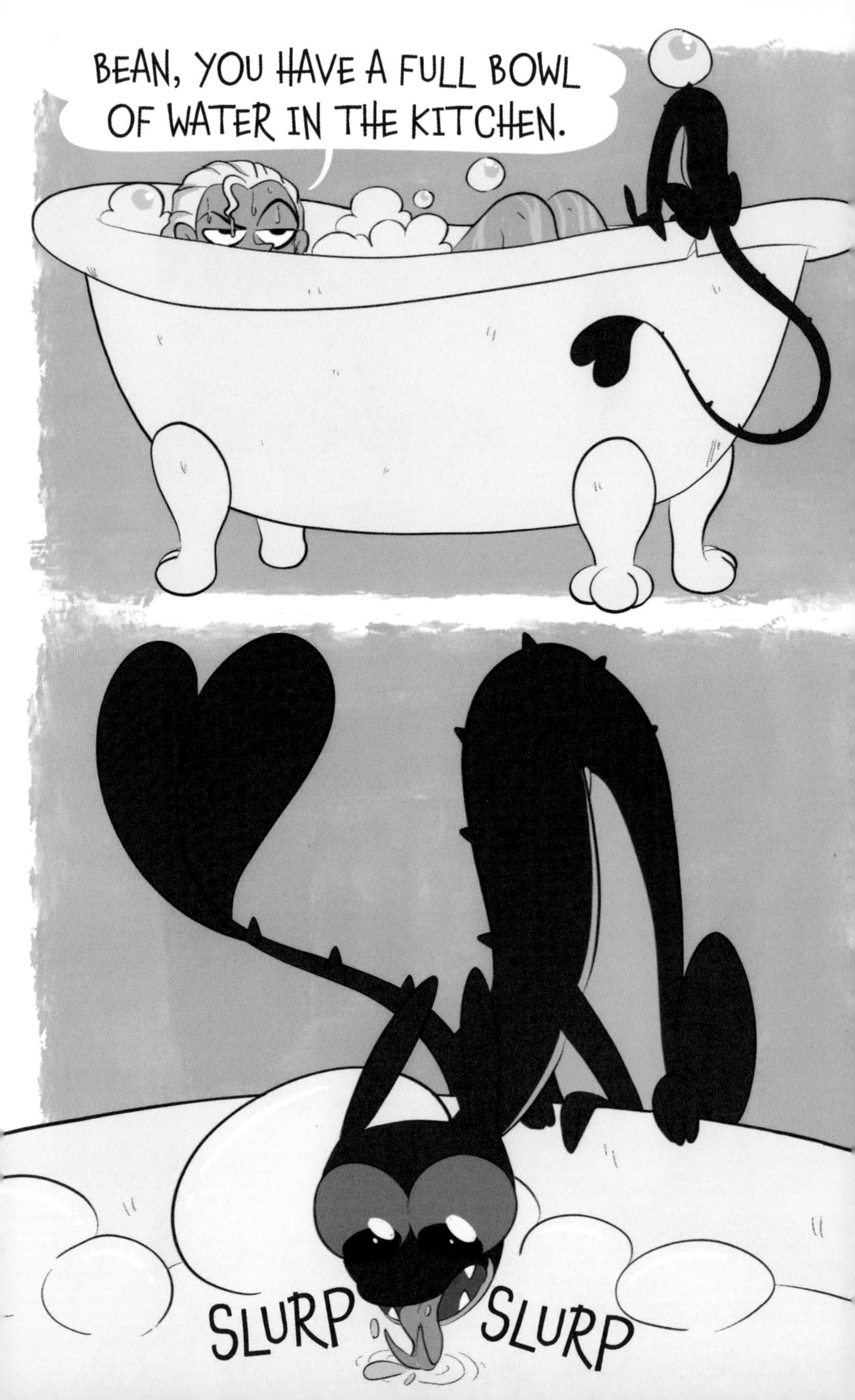
BEAN, YOU HAVE A FULL BOWL OF WATER IN THE KITCHEN.
SLURP SLURP

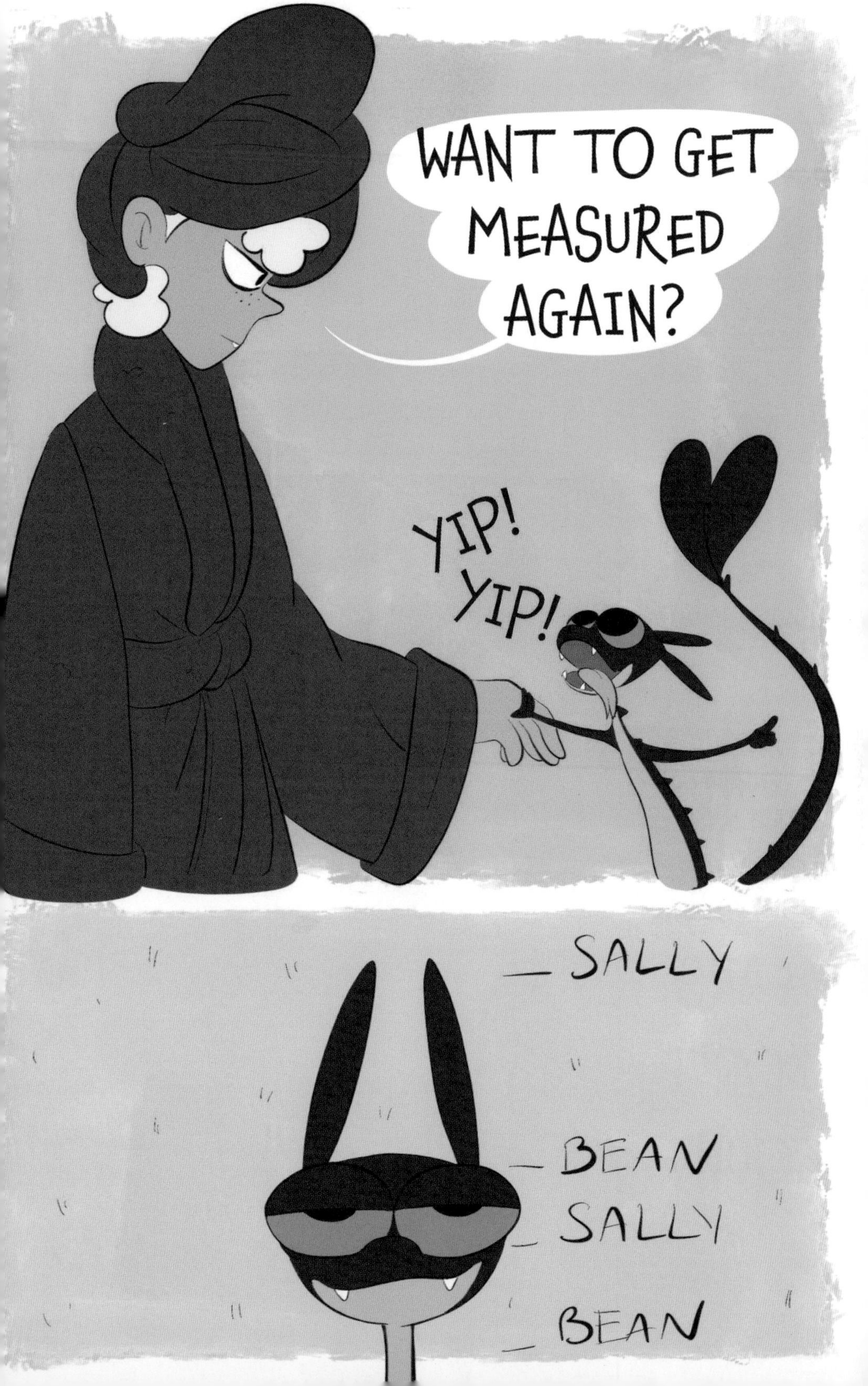
WANT TO GET MEASURED AGAIN?
YIP! YIP!
SALLY
BEAN
SALLY
BEAN

SALLY
SALLY
BEAN
SALLY
BEAN
BEAN
BEAN
SORRY BEAN, EARS DON'T COUNT.

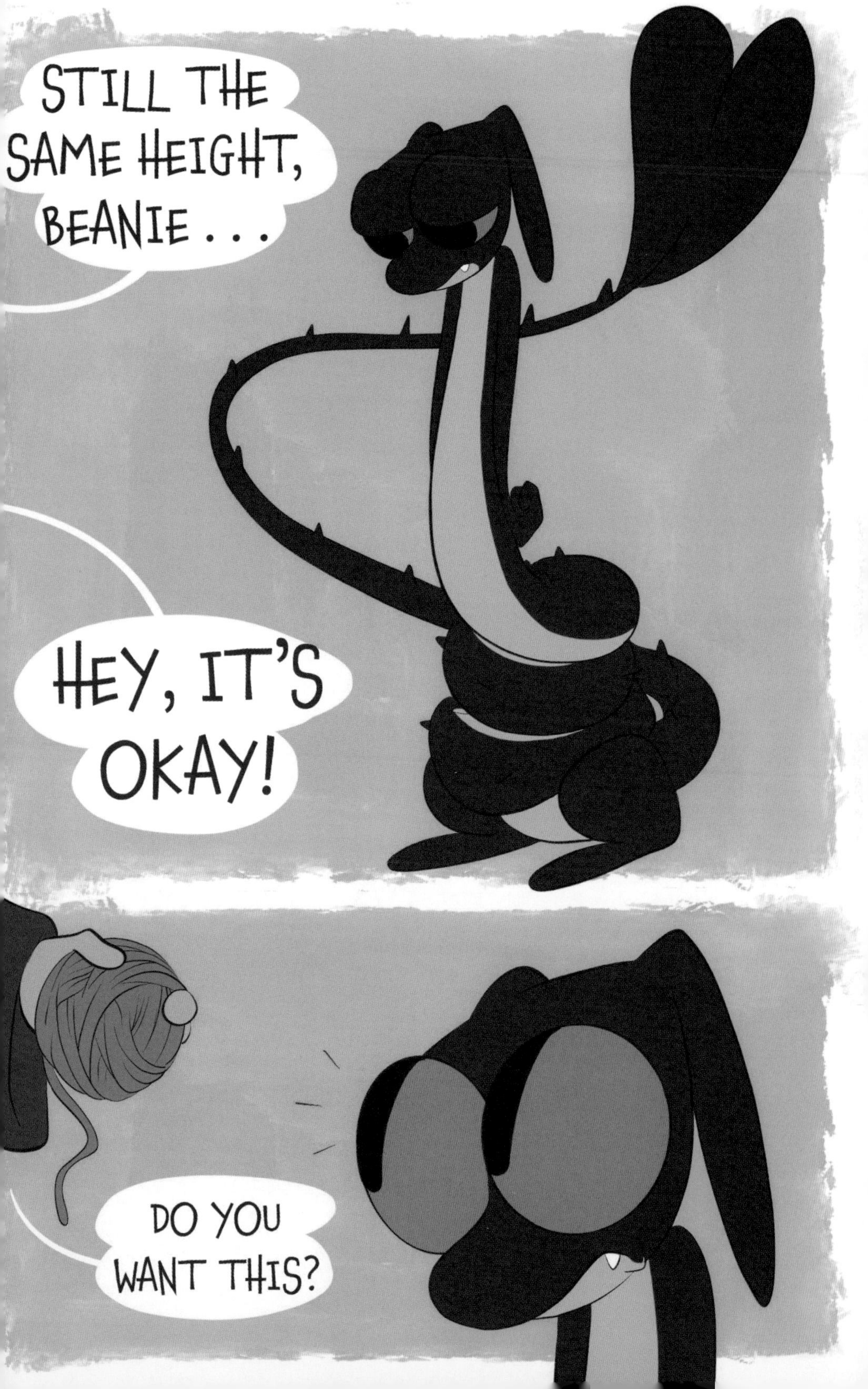
STILL THE SAME HEIGHT, BEANIE . . .
HEY, IT'S OKAY!
DO YOU WANT THIS?

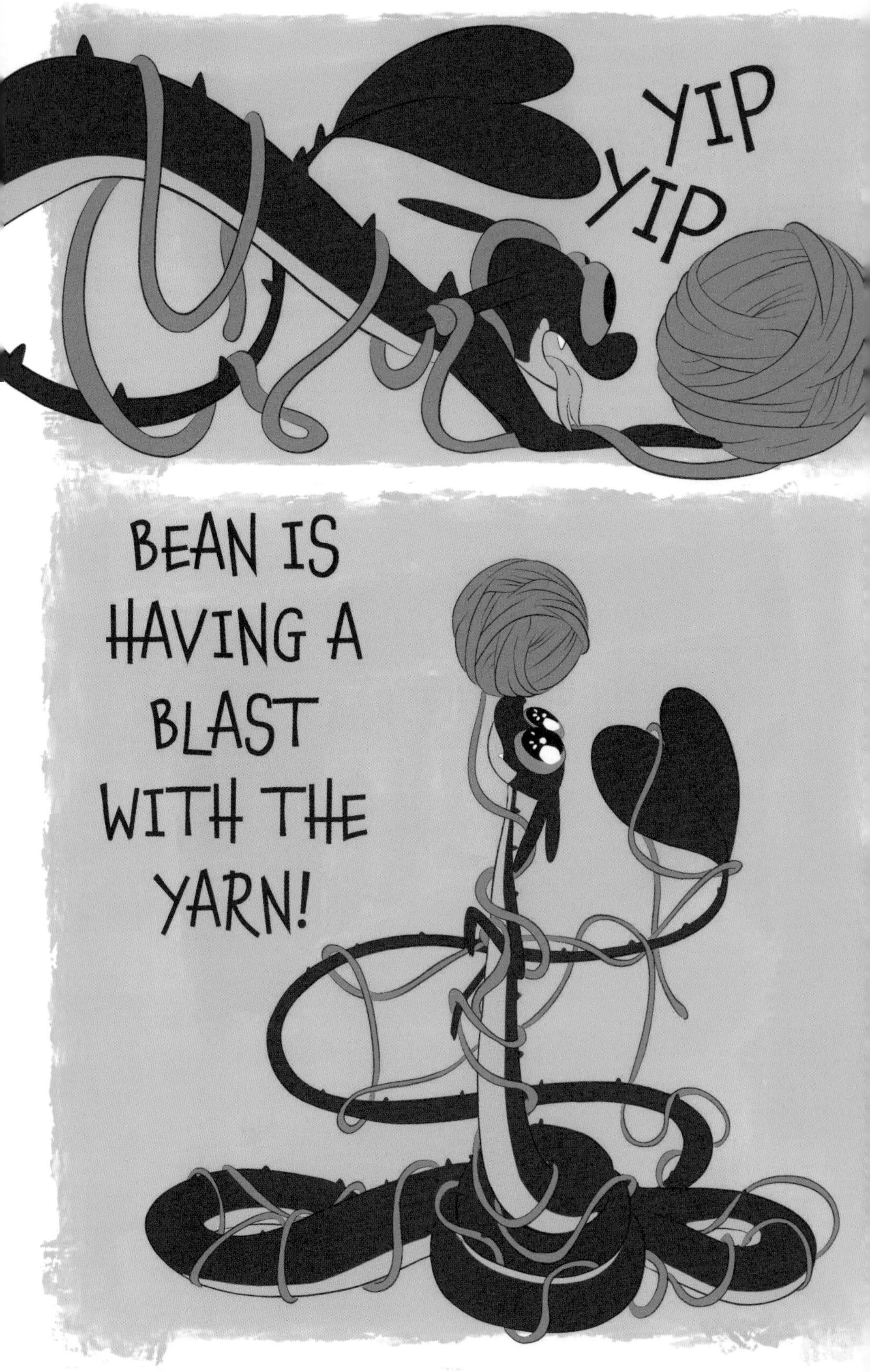
YIP
YIP
BEAN IS HAVING A BLAST WITH THE YARN!

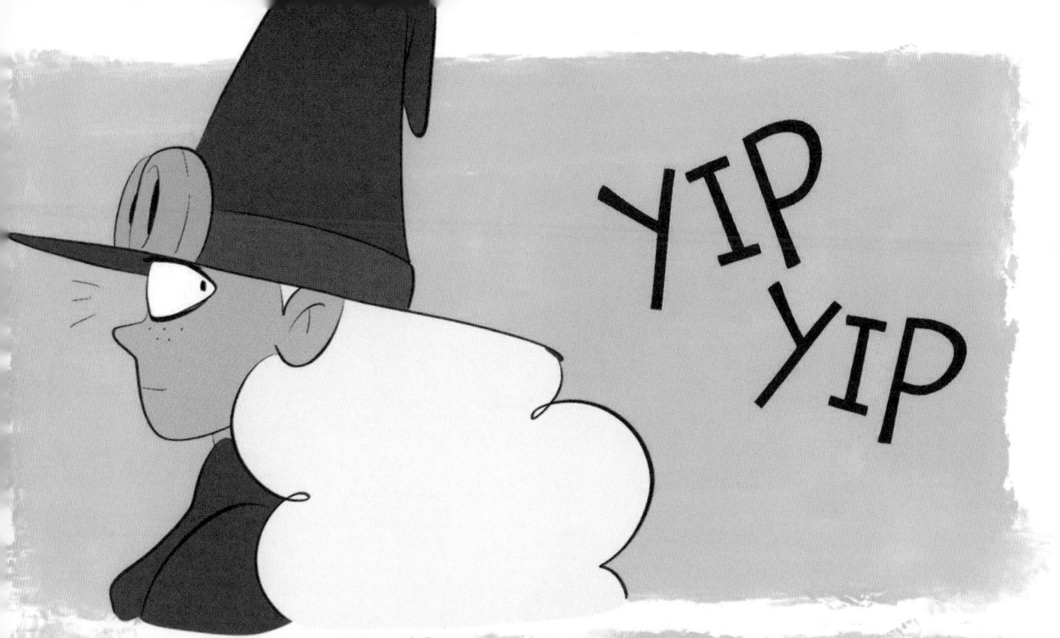
YIP
YIP

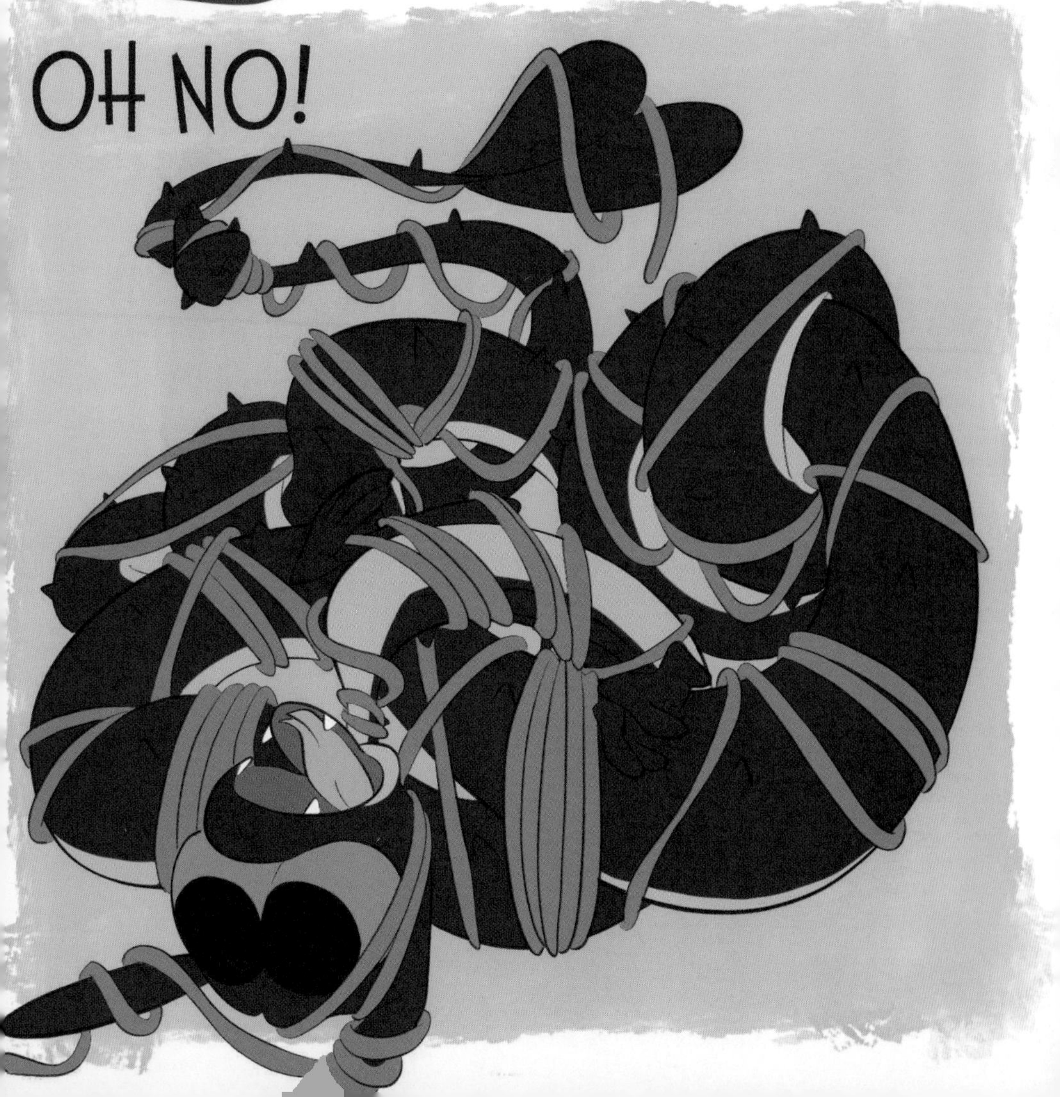
OH NO!

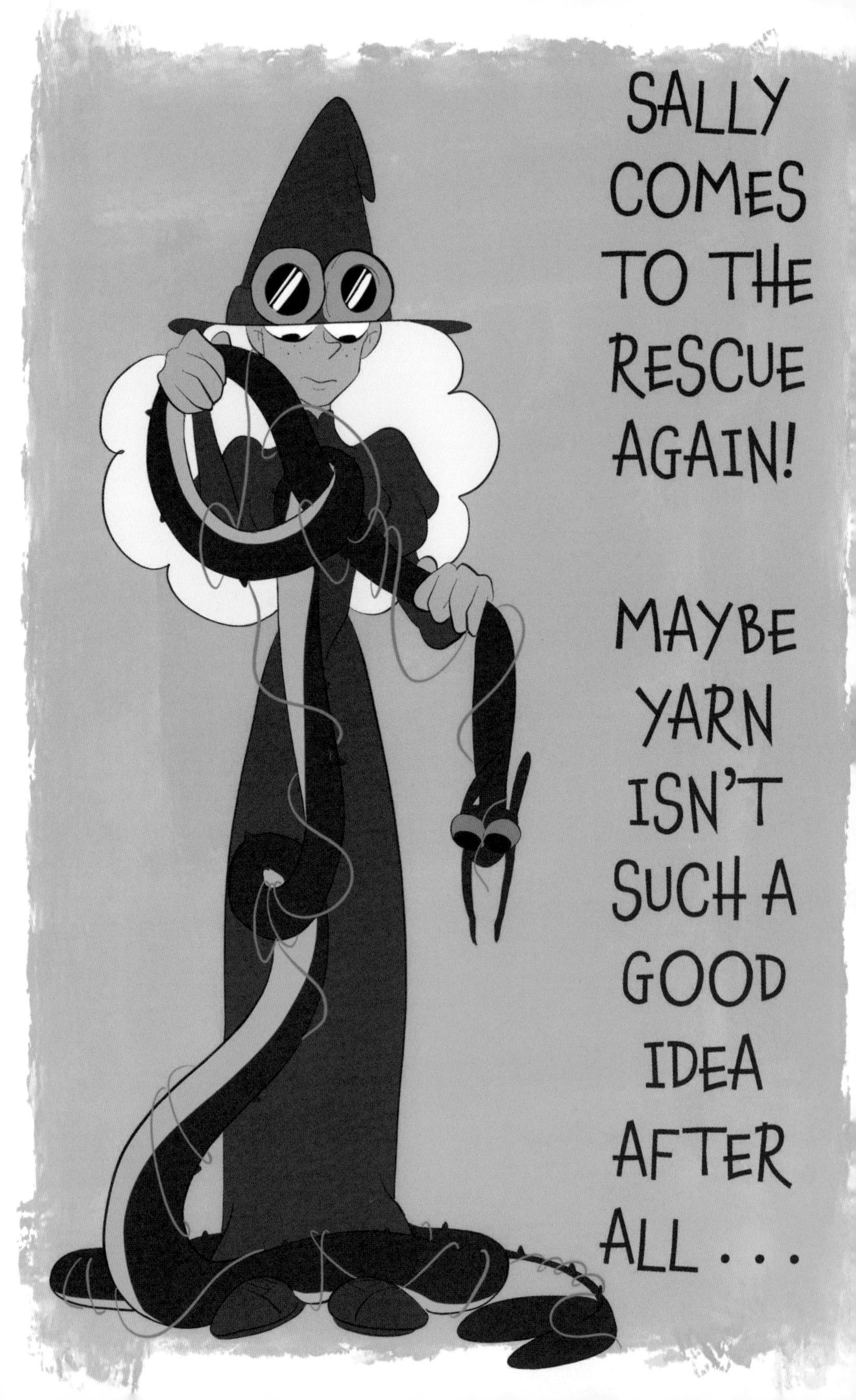

SALLY COMES TO THE RESCUE AGAIN!

MAYBE YARN ISN'T SUCH A GOOD IDEA AFTER ALL . . .

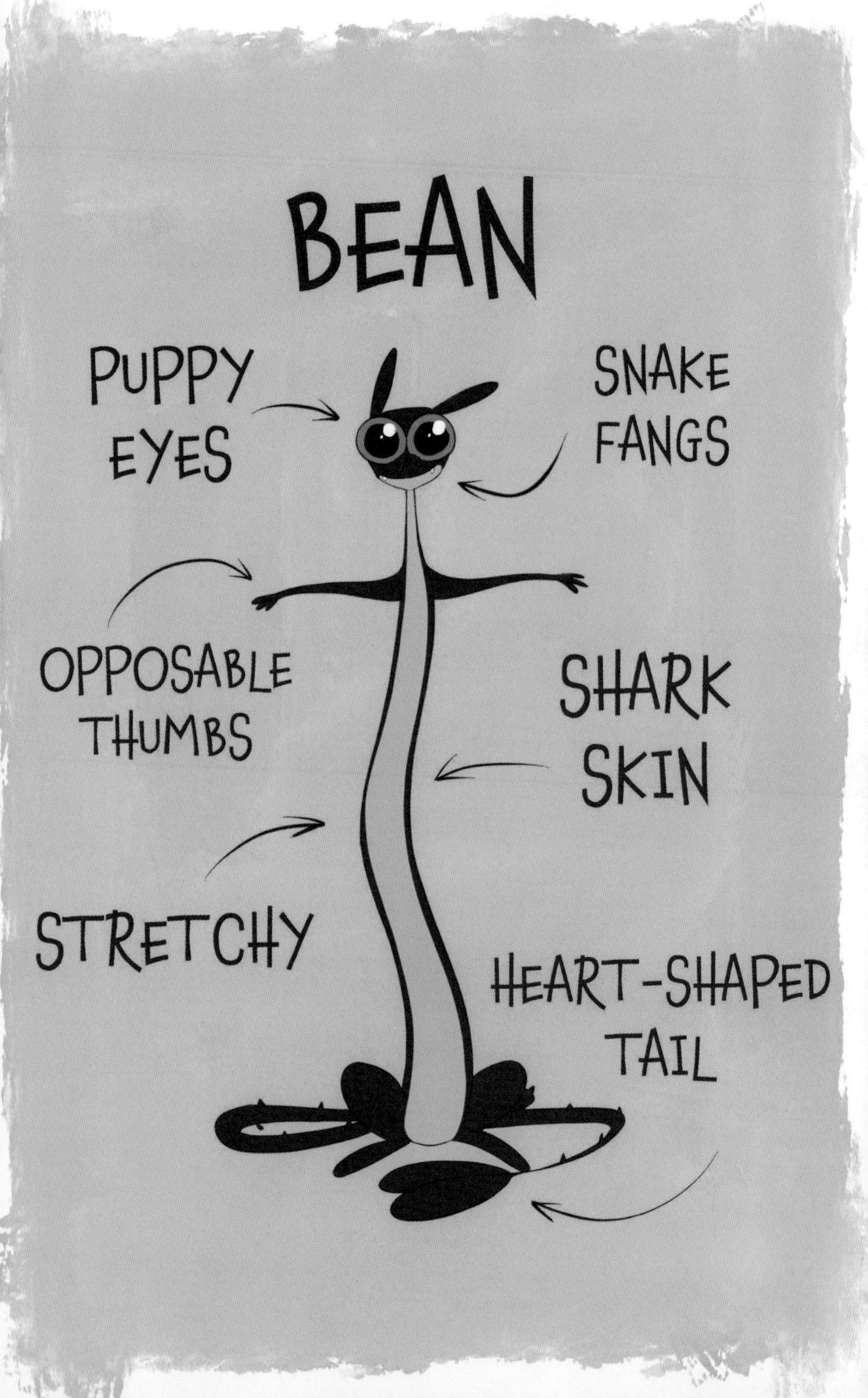
BEAN
PUPPY EYES
SNAKE FANGS
OPPOSABLE THUMBS
SHARK SKIN
STRETCHY
HEART-SHAPED TAIL

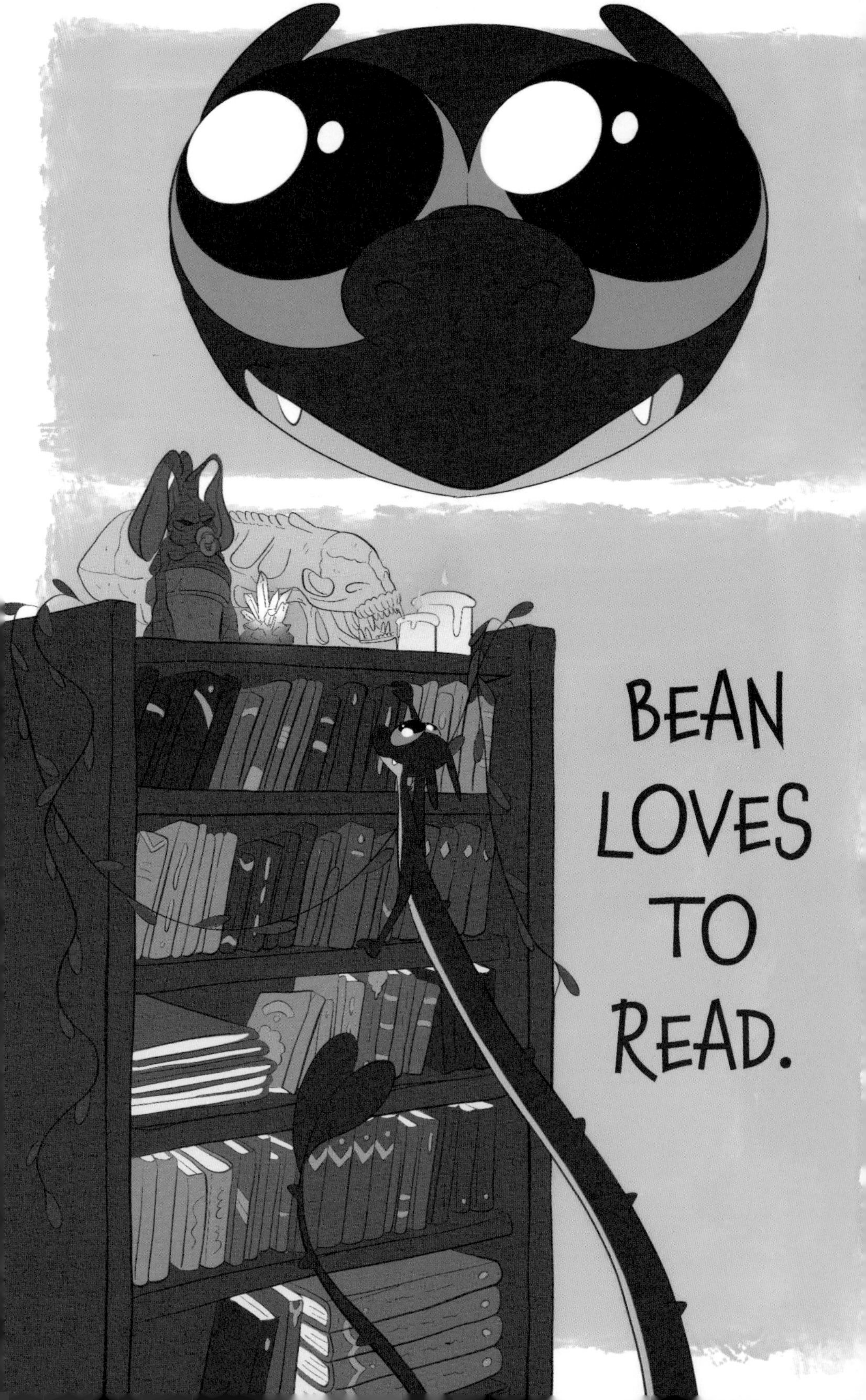
BEAN LOVES TO READ.

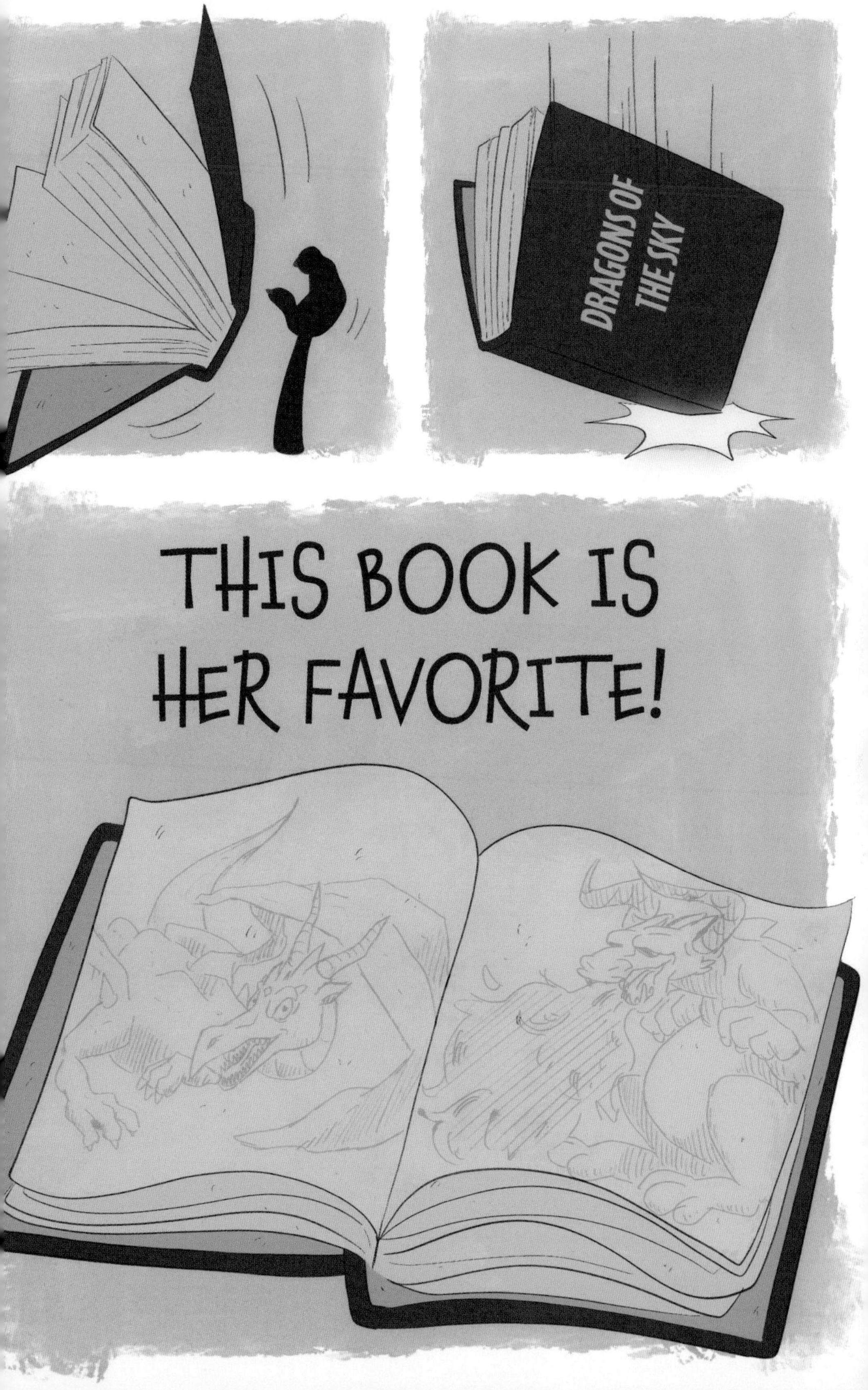
DRAGONS OF THE SKY
THIS BOOK IS HER FAVORITE!

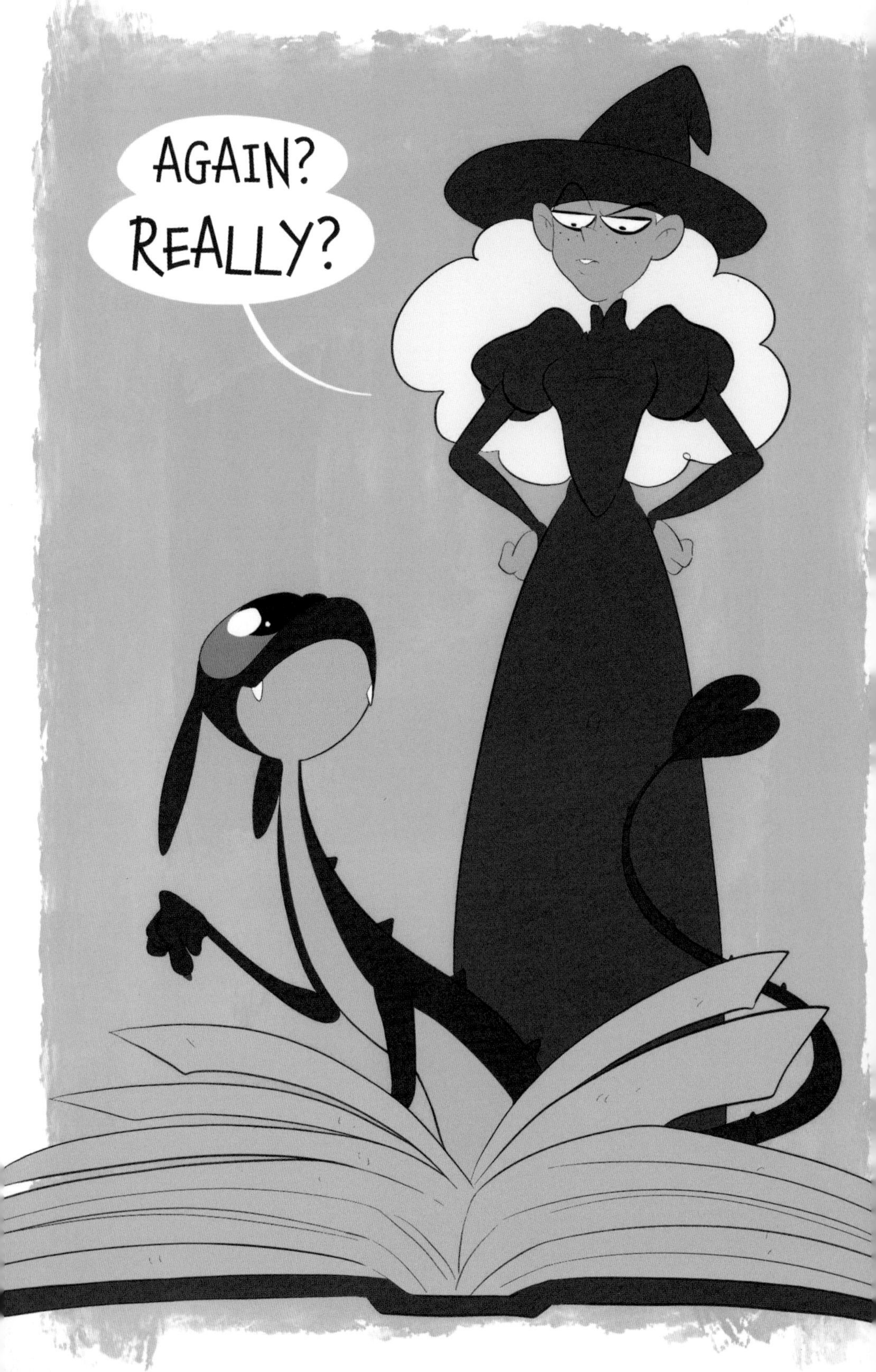
AGAIN? REALLY?

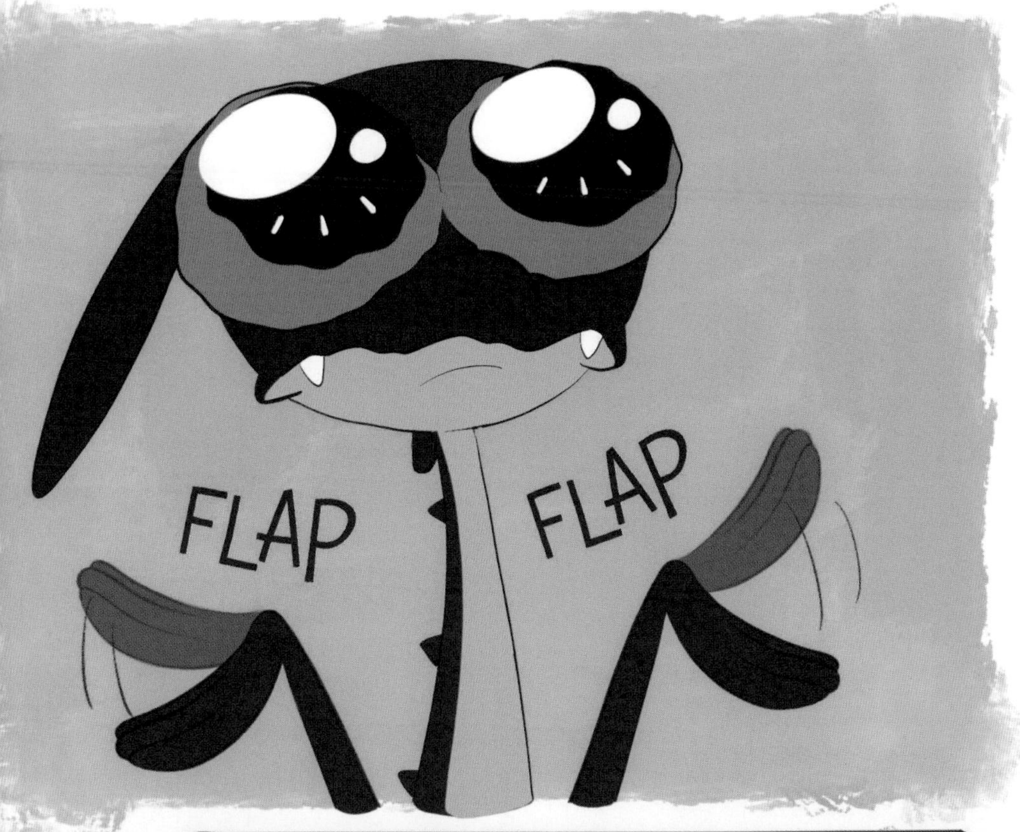
FLAP
FLAP
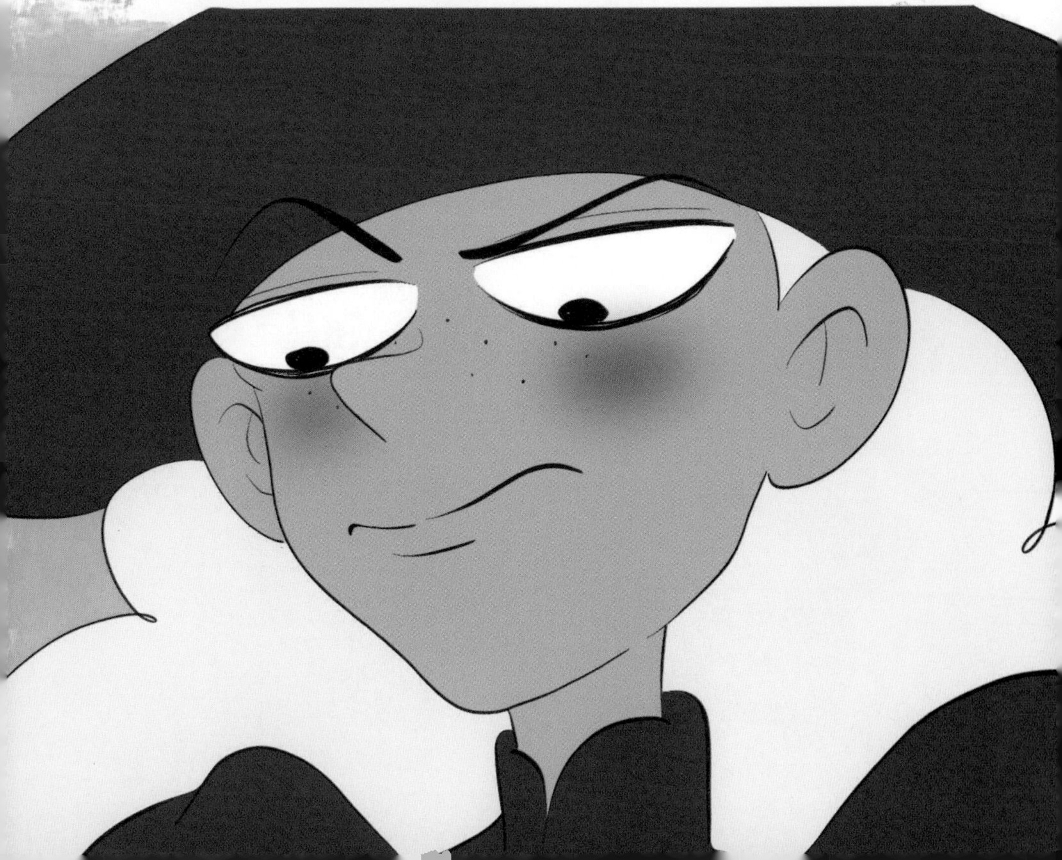

READING HER FAVORITE BOOK ALWAYS INSPIRES A FLIGHT SESSION.

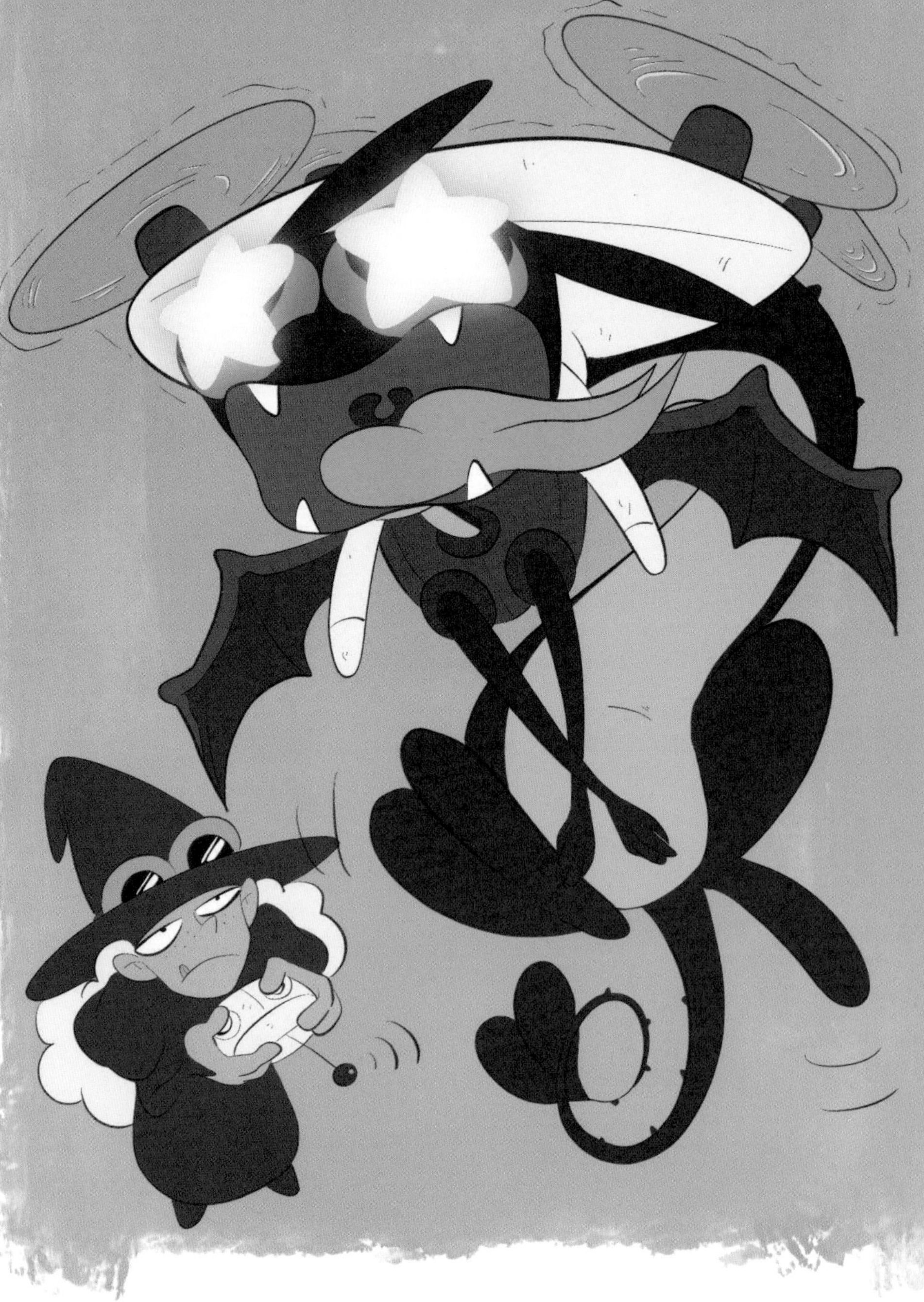

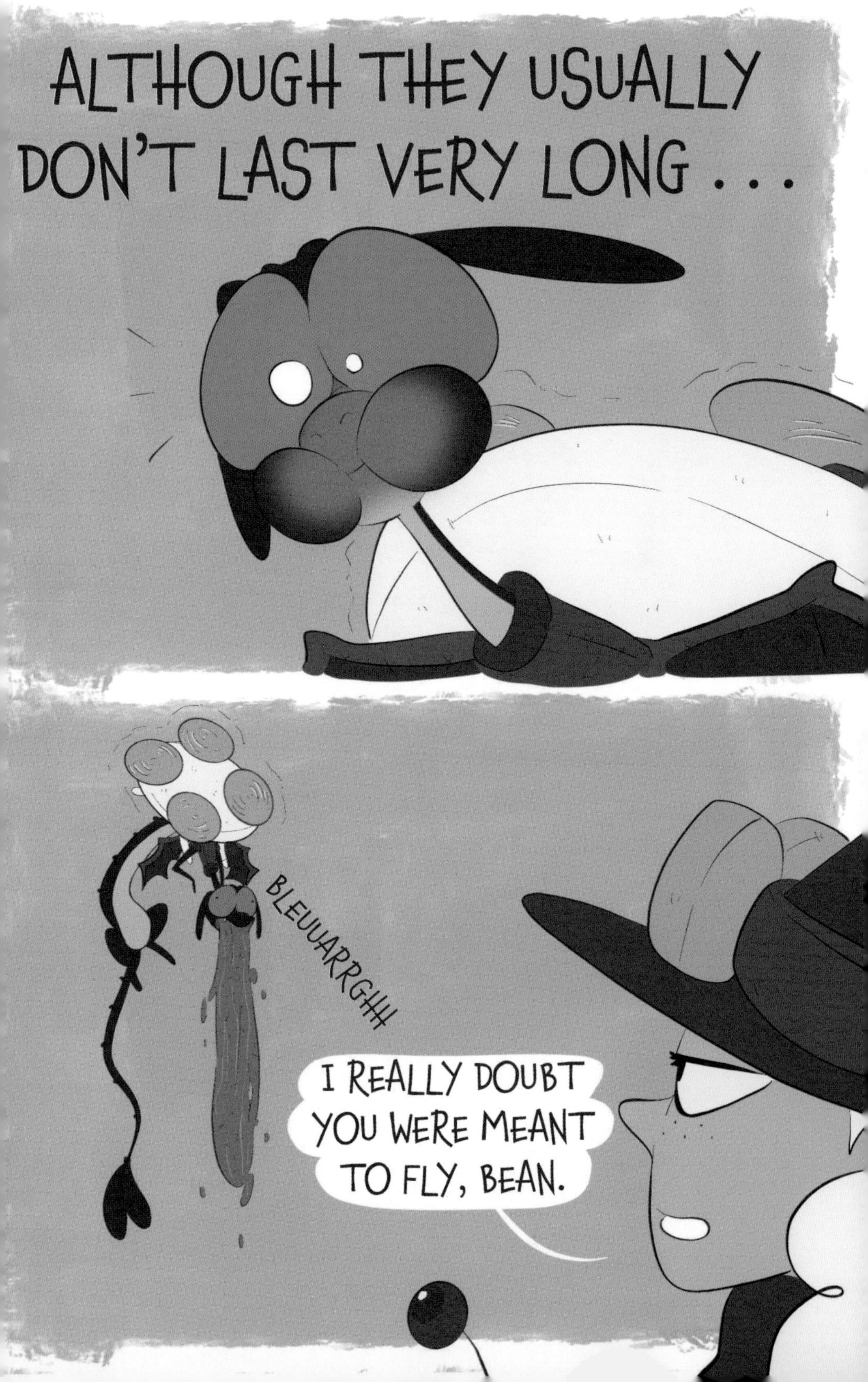
ALTHOUGH THEY USUALLY DON'T LAST VERY LONG . . .
BLEUUARRGHH
I REALLY DOUBT YOU WERE MEANT TO FLY, BEAN.

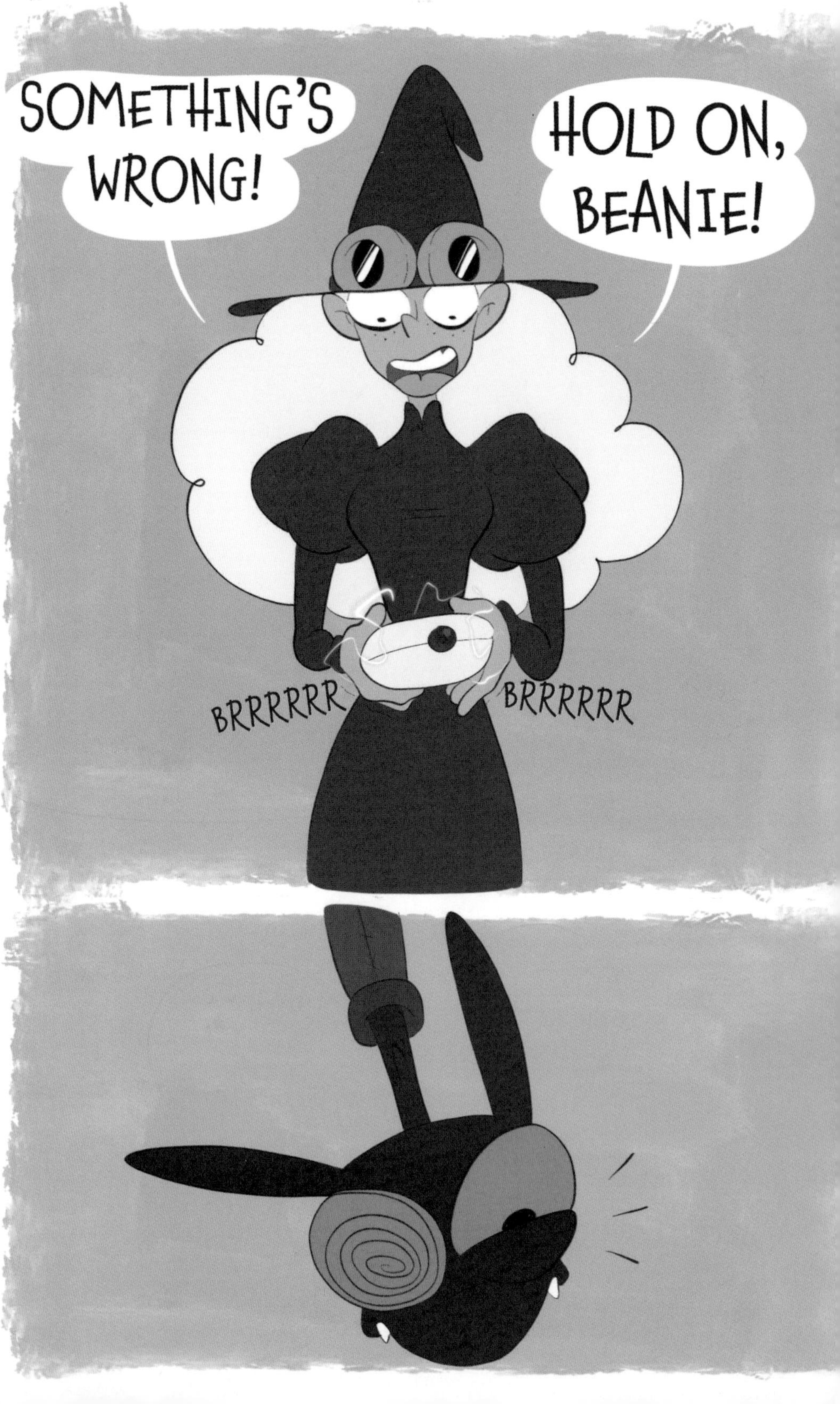
SOMETHING'S WRONG!
HOLD ON, BEANIE!
BRRRRRR
BRRRRRR

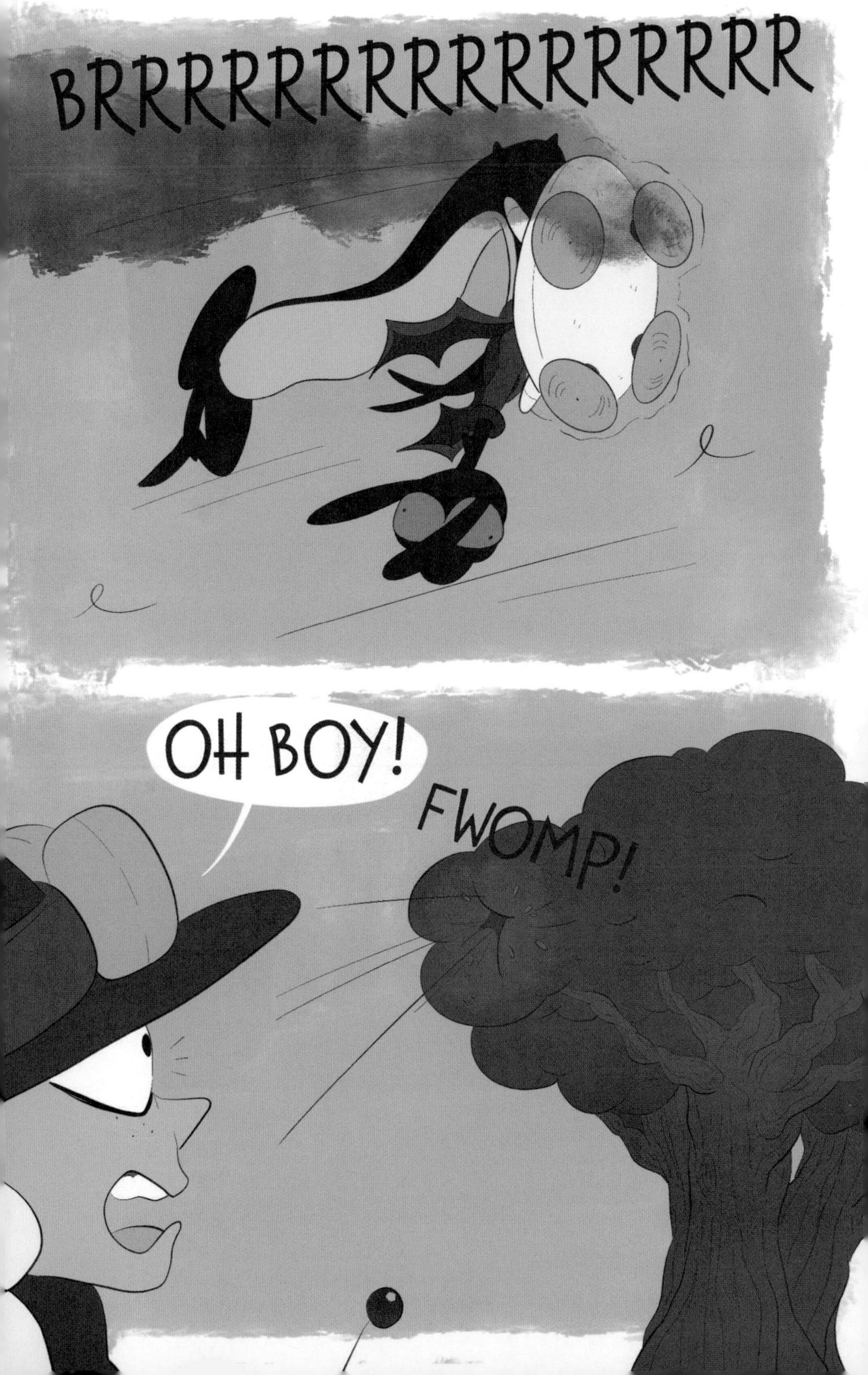
BRRRRRRRRRRRRRRRR
OH BOY!
FWOMP!

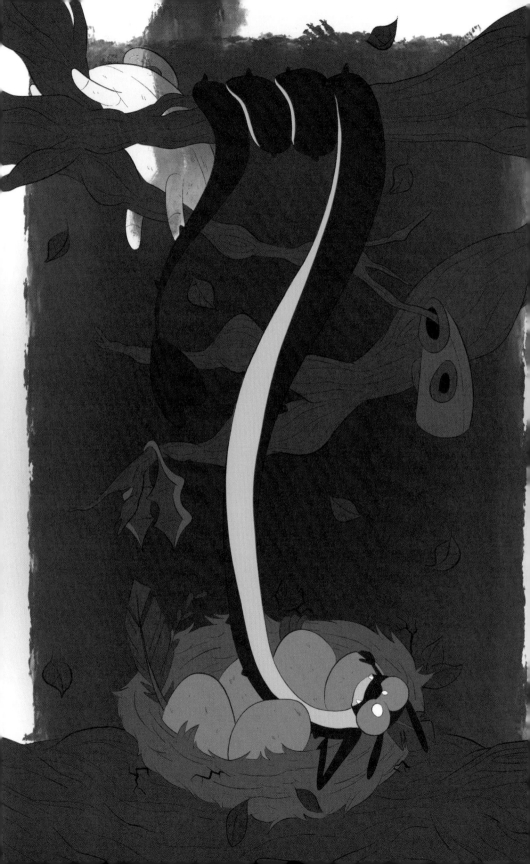

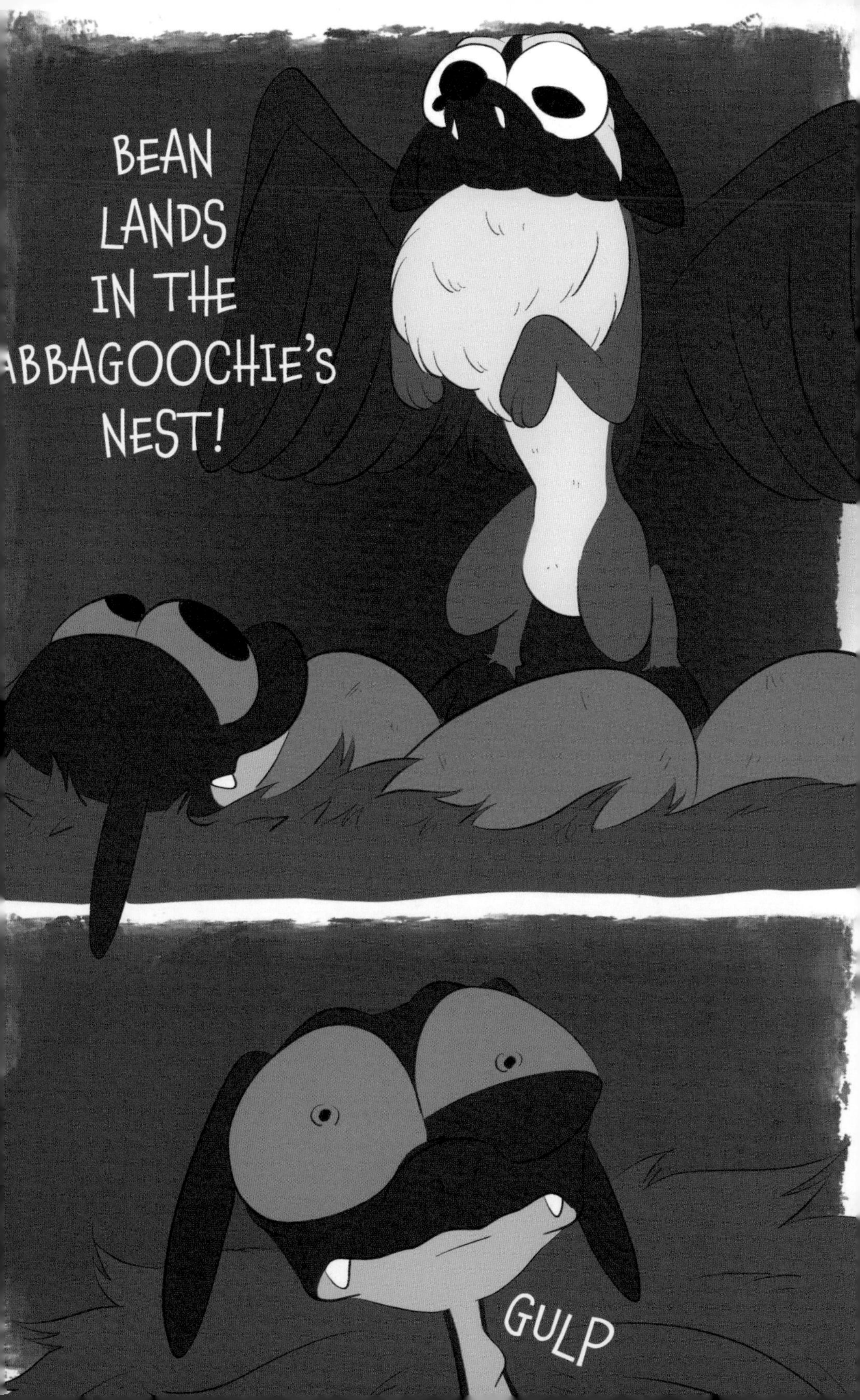
BEAN LANDS IN THE ABBAGOOCHIE'S NEST!
GULP

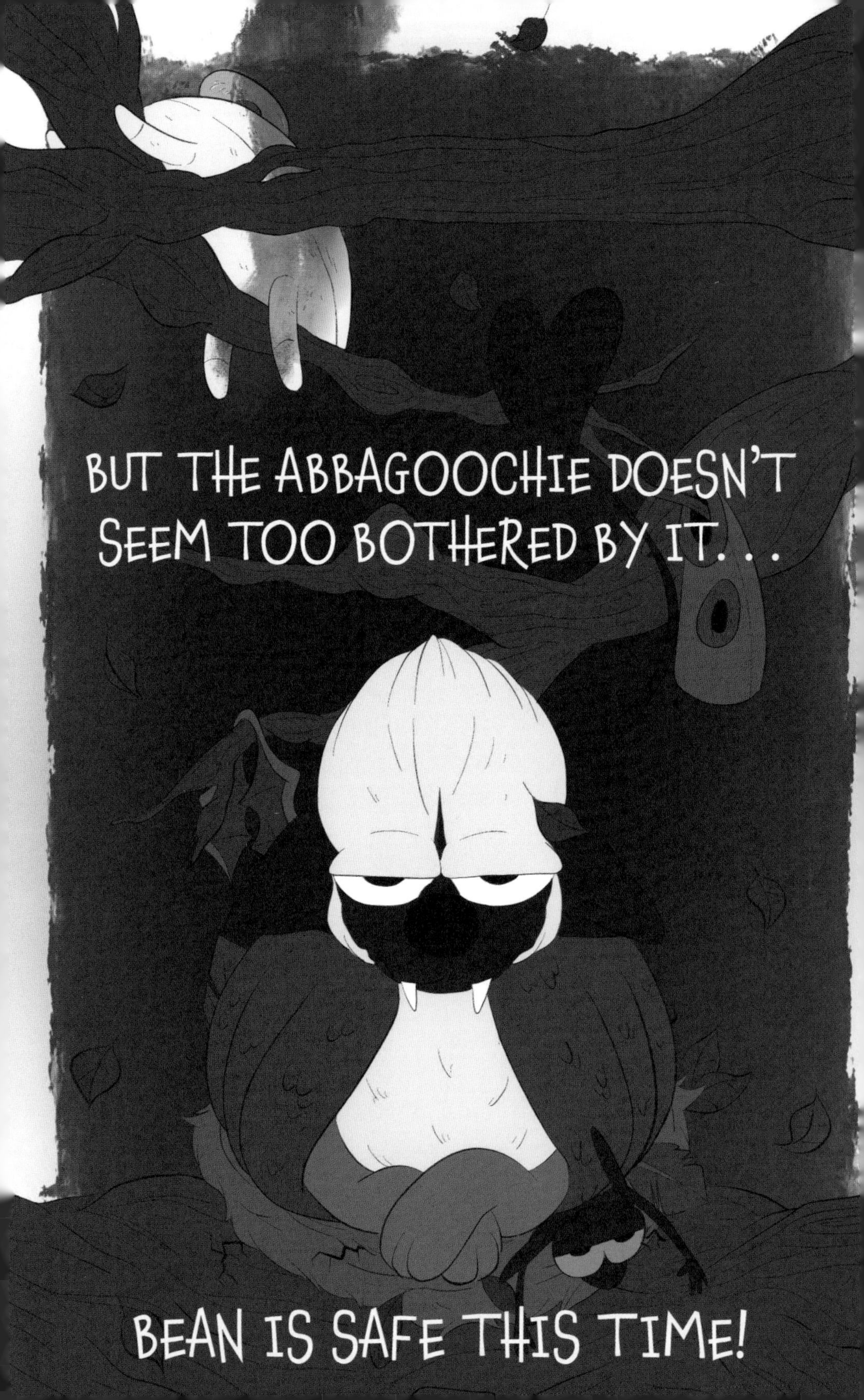
BUT THE ABBAGOOCHIE DOESN'T SEEM TOO BOTHERED BY IT. . .
BEAN IS SAFE THIS TIME!

THE ABBAGOOCHIE

FOX FACE

OWL WINGS

DEER HOOVES

A mix between an owl, a fox, and a deer, they are known for their incredible appetite, being able to eat other animals four times their size like horses and cows! They will even eat their own eggs, which they lay every six years, in order to protect them.

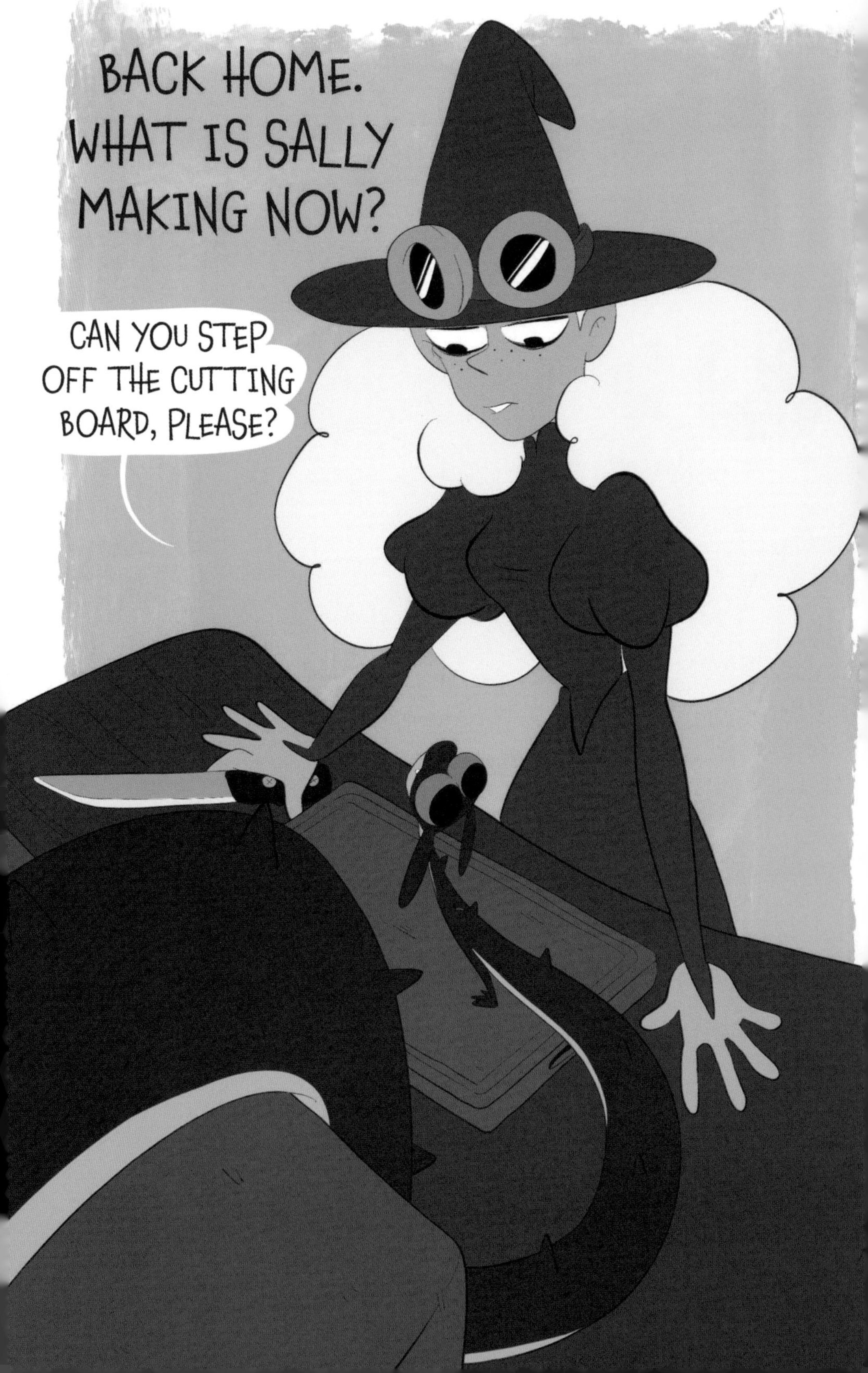
BACK HOME. WHAT IS SALLY MAKING NOW?
CAN YOU STEP OFF THE CUTTING BOARD, PLEASE?

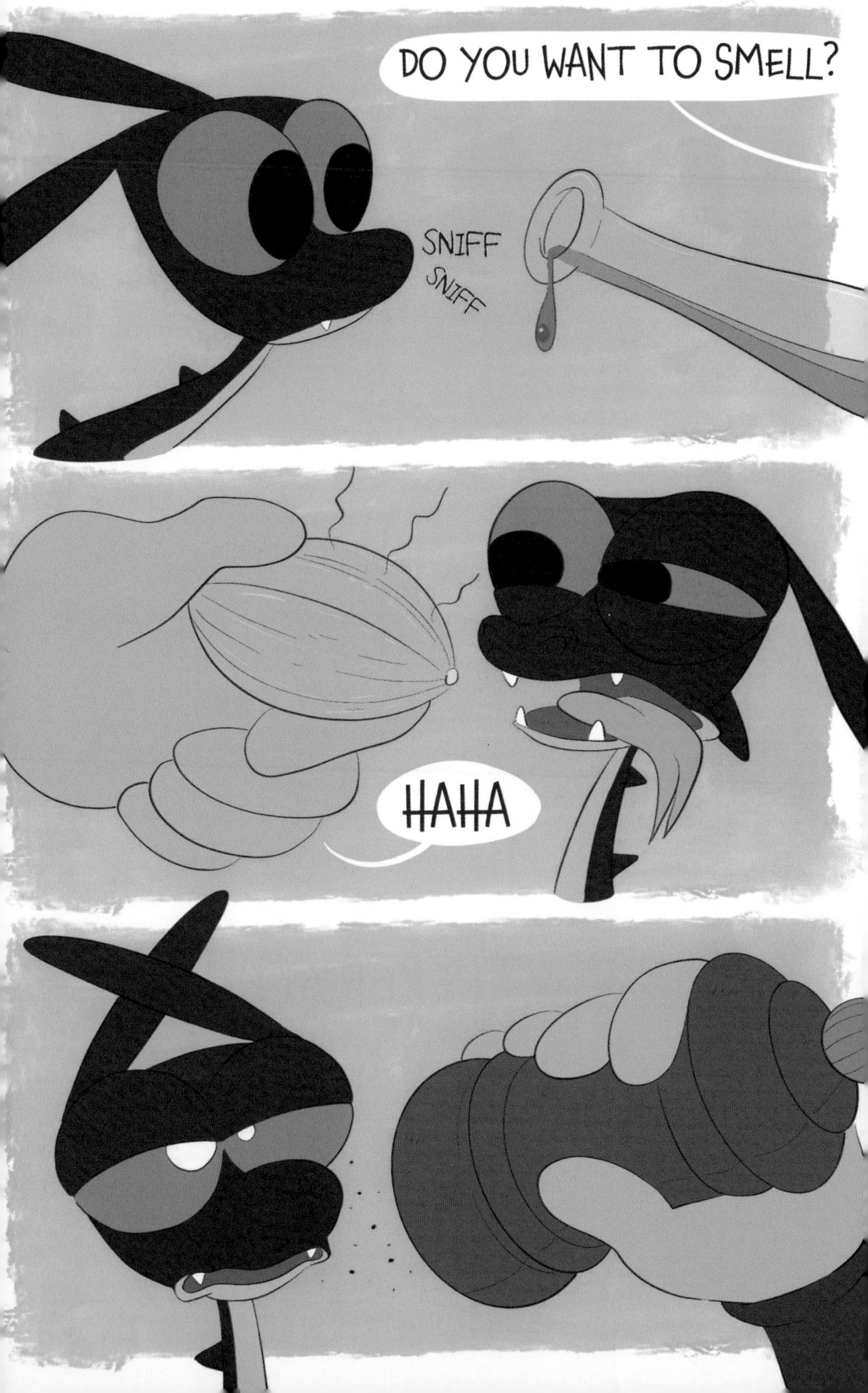
DO YOU WANT TO SMELL?
SNIFF
SNIFF
HAHA

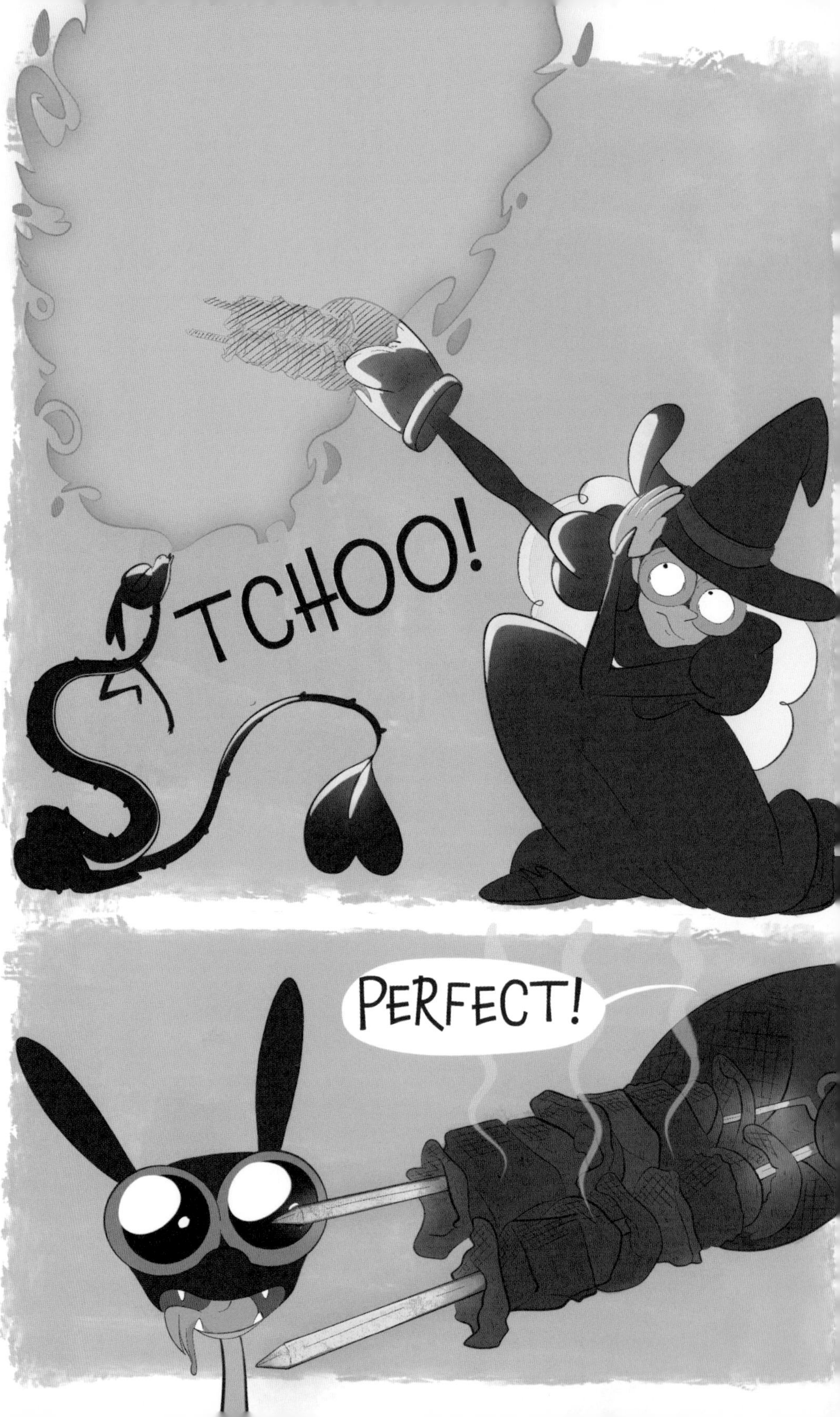
TCHOO!
PERFECT!

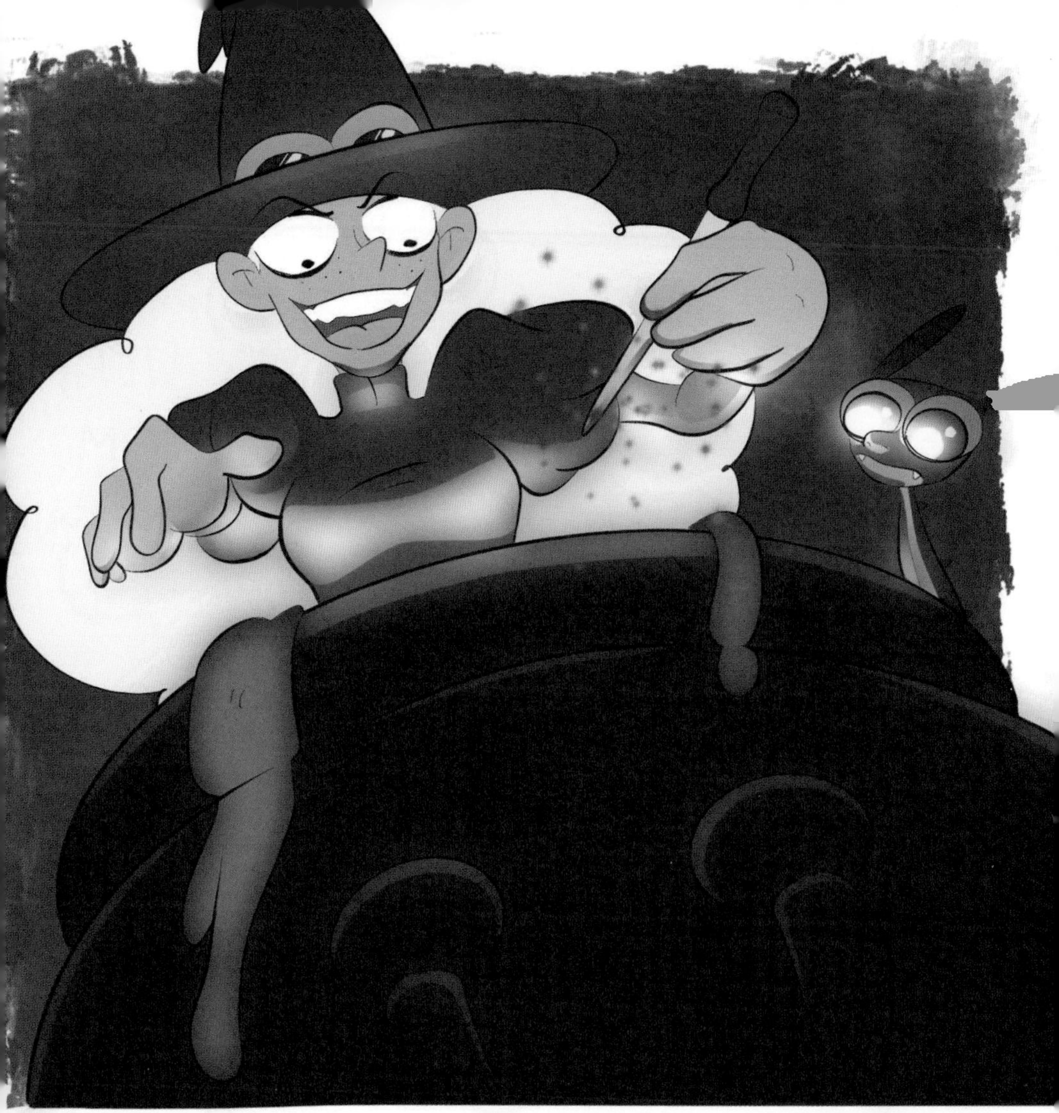

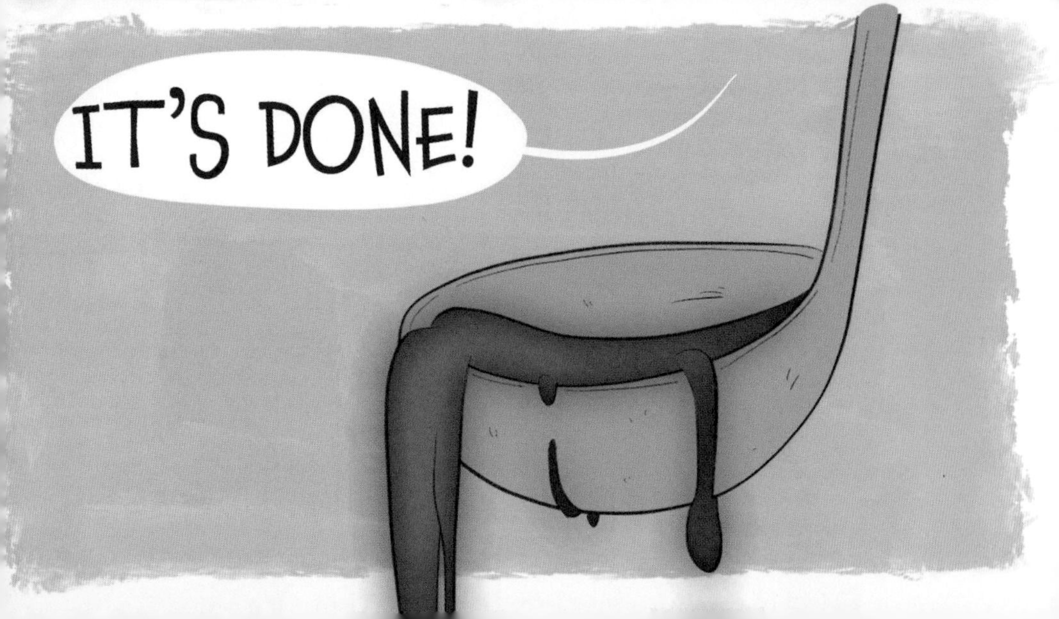
IT'S DONE!

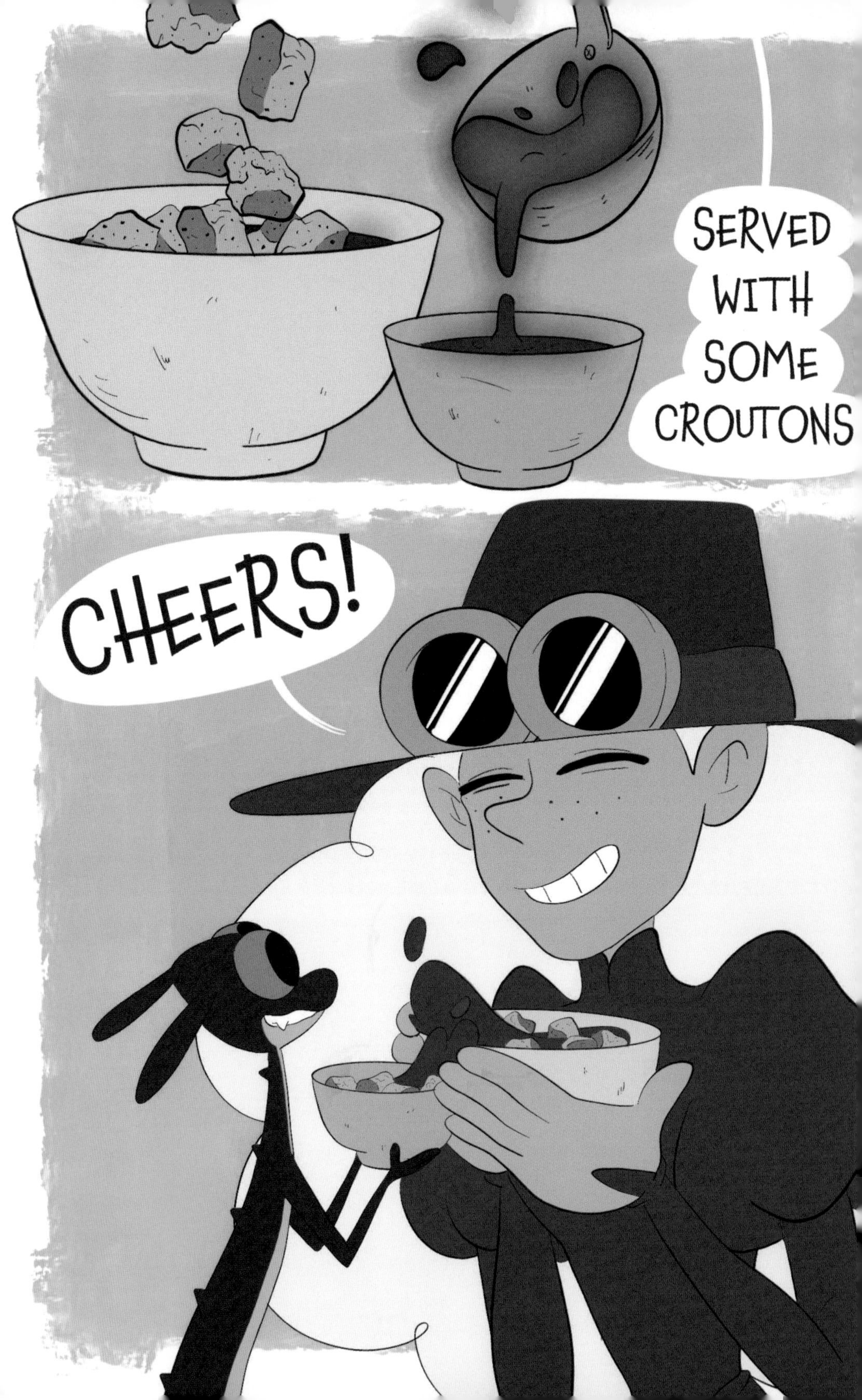
SERVED WITH SOME CROUTONS
CHEERS!

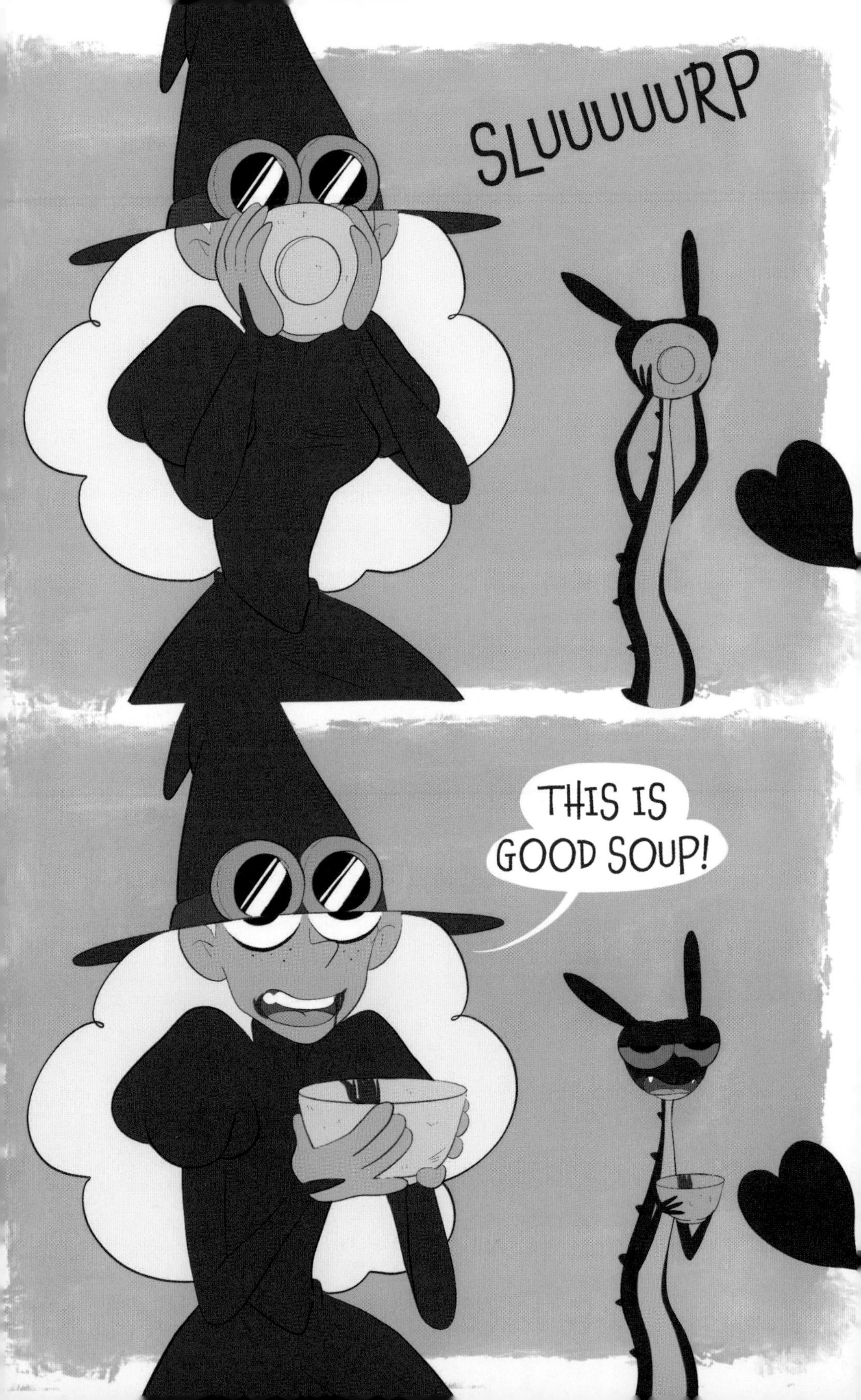
SLUUUUURP
THIS IS GOOD SOUP!

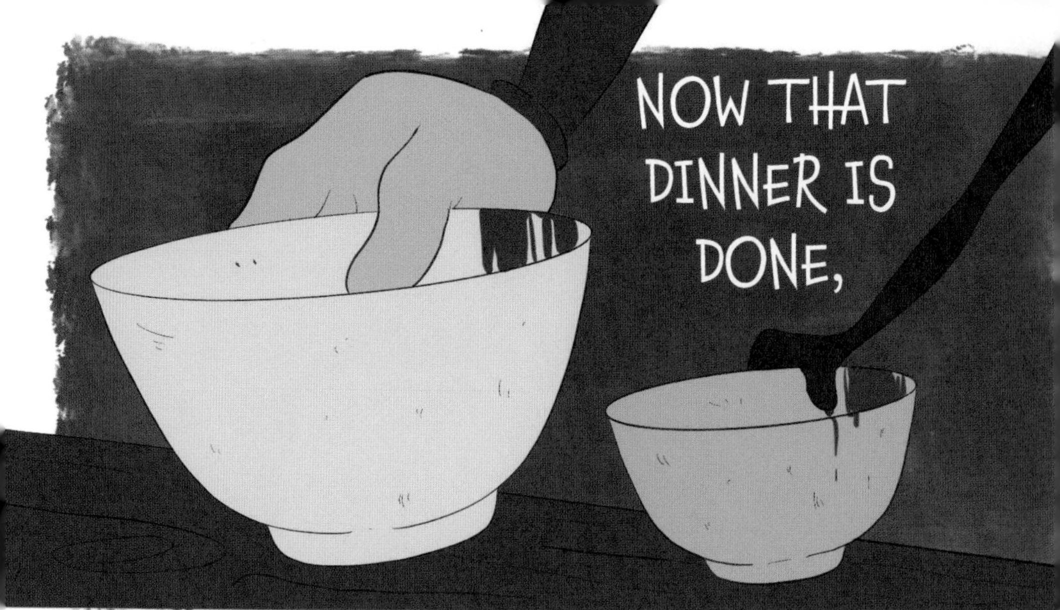
NOW THAT DINNER IS DONE,

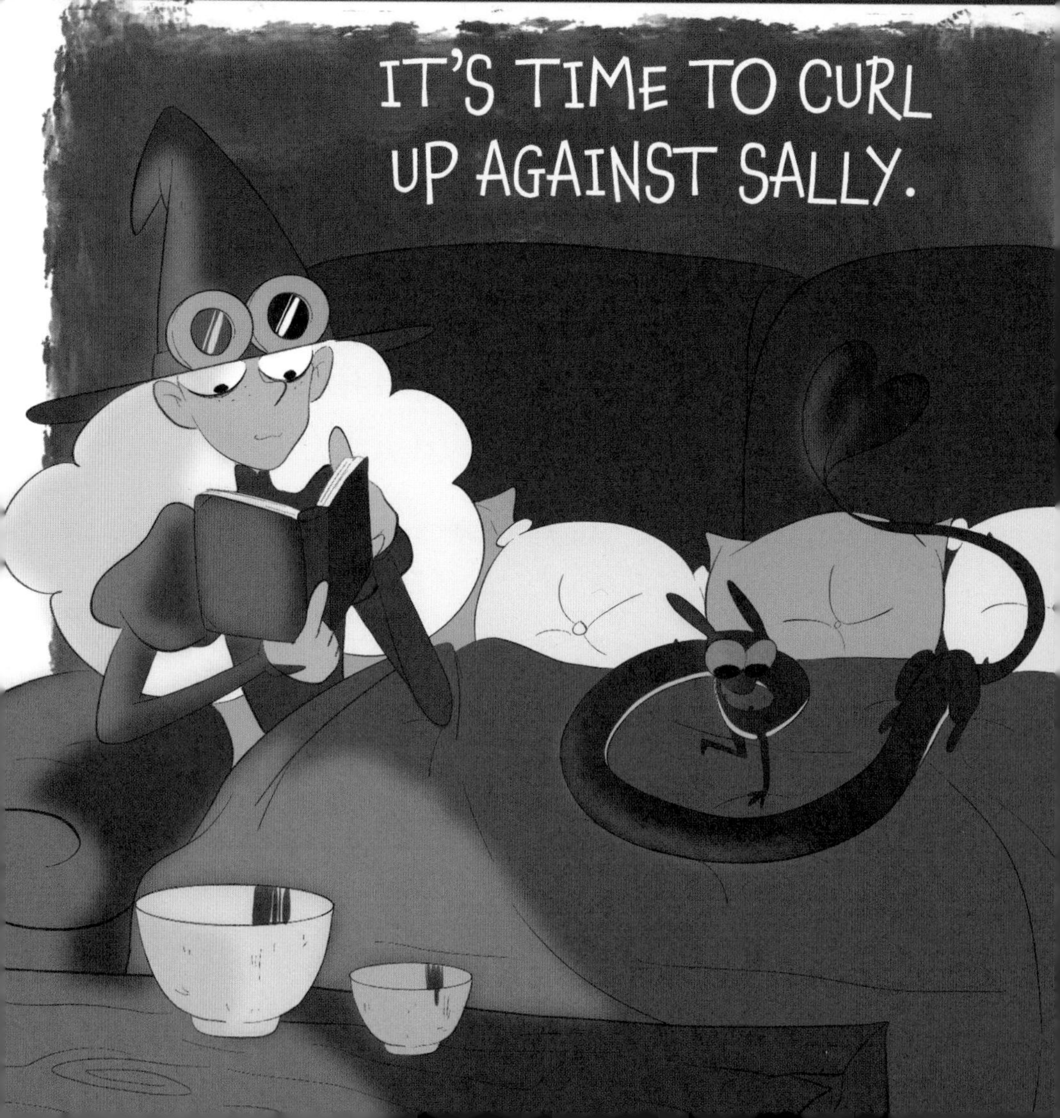
IT'S TIME TO CURL UP AGAINST SALLY.

AND, AFTER A
LONG DAY, FINALLY
FALL ASLEEP BY
THE FIRE, UNTIL
TOMORROW COMES!

Andrews McMeel Publishing
a division of Andrews McMeel Universal
1130 Walnut Street, Kansas City, Missouri 64106

www.andrewsmcmeel.com

23 24 25 26 27 SDB 10 9 8 7 6 5 4 3 2 1

ISBN: 978-1-5248-8101-6

Library of Congress Control Number: 2023931030

Editor: Hannah Dussold
Art Director: Holly Swayne
Production Editor: Brianna Westervelt
Production Manager: Julie Skalla

Made by:
RR Donnelley (Guangdong) Printing Solutions Company Ltd
Address and location of manufacturer:
No. 2, Minzhu Road, Daning, Humen Town,
Dongguan City, Guangdong Province, China 523930
1st Printing – 04/24/2023